# A BABY FOR THE LUMBERJACKS

## CHLOE KENT

BLUSHING BOOKS

Published by Blushing Books®,
a subsidiary of
ABCD Graphics and Design
977 Seminole Trail #233
Charlottesville, VA 22901
The trademark Blushing Books®
is registered in the US Patent and Trademark Office.

Chloe Kent
A Baby for the Lumberjacks

EBook ISBN: 978-1-61258-432-4
Print ISBN: 978-1-61258-971-8

Cover Art by ABCD Graphics & Design
Version 1.2

# CHAPTER 1

*Oh, Dad, what have you done?*

Saffron Sinclair stared at her father in complete disbelief. Maybe she had heard him incorrectly. Maybe she was having a very strange nightmarish-kind of dream right this minute and was not really in their little kitchen with the yellow polka dot curtains and turquoise chairs her mother had loved so much. This could not be happening.

"You did what?" she asked again. She needed her father to repeat the warped thing he had just uttered seconds ago so he could follow it with a *just kidding* laugh.

"Red, it's okay. It needed to be done. It's the only way out and finally we'll be free of all these dark clouds hanging over our heads. Dad did the only thing he could do."

Saffron turned her head in the direction of her sister, Marigold, a picture of perfection with her sunshine blonde hair pulled into a neat bun and her brown eyes wide and innocent. Dressed in a pale pink sweater and tweed knee-length skirt, she looked fragile and sweet. She hugged an orange coffee mug between her fingers as was her custom and Saffron felt the familiar surge of protectiveness she always felt for her twenty-two-year-old sister who was a year older than Saffron.

"Are you serious?" Saffron cried. "Goldy, what Dad did is unthinkably low and I can't believe... I can't believe you're okay with this." She swung her attention back to her father, the real culprit here, not Marigold. "Dad, you have to give them the money back."

"You know I can't do that. You don't go back on your word with those types of men." Alan Sinclair lowered his head and fiddled with the paint peeling off the yellow wooden kitchen table. A moment of guilt washed over her as he bowed his head, ageing right before her eyes.

Ugh! How could everything be so fucking unfair? How did they end up here with this mess on their heads? Oh, yes. Her mother passed away five years ago from cancer and to keep their struggling family restaurant afloat, her father had taken out loans against everything they owned—which was meager to start off with. And when he poured everything into the restaurant only to have it fail epically, his frustration had caused him to revert to a habit he had kicked fifteen years ago. Gambling.

He'd stopped caring about his daughters, and the restaurant. He gambled away money they didn't have and played with really bad people who had broken their windows in the middle of night, and then his wrists because he hadn't paid them back yet.

When that happened three months ago, he had confided in his daughters, weeping at the stupid mistakes he had made, the shady business deals he had been threatened into doing, and the kind of people he had become involved with. He had begged their forgiveness. Saffron and Marigold had done so immediately. But Saffron knew that without her mother there to set their father straight, he would be the man he'd been when they were so much younger. He would lie, cheat, and steal for his gambling habit.

Saffron came up with a plan to simply leave New York altogether and start all over again somewhere else. Anywhere else. But her father had told them they would never be safe. Those thugs he associated with would find them, and hurt them. And then there were the banks who would be after him, too.

What a mess.

Marigold had to drop out of school where she'd been studying for a prestigious degree in art because there were no more funds to pay for her education. Saffron had to work three jobs as a waitress just to feed them now. They were going to lose the house to the banks, just as they had the restaurant. And now possibly their lives were at stake, too.

But her father had loved her mother, and losing the house meant losing her all over again. He just hadn't been the same since her death and Saffron couldn't blame him. That was when he'd told them everything, when the house was going to be taken from them and with his wrists in casts after the crime thug had broken them. He'd wept pitifully then.

Saffron paced the floor, biting her lips and shaking her head every five seconds. She really had to stop asking how they'd gotten to this point—it happened the moment her mother died, their lives had gone downhill with no hope at all.

But there must be a way for her to stop this from happening and still save their house and pay off the thugs her father owed. Panic at her hopelessness and helplessness tormented her. She usually excelled at being resourceful and came up with solutions quickly.

"I don't mind, Red," Marigold said softly. "It could have been worse. I met them and even though I wasn't sure which one it was going to be, they looked handsome and decent. I think I can do this."

"What? Marigold, a few months ago you were studying art, you were going to be a famous painter, and now suddenly you're all on board with this? Are you serious?"

"We don't have a choice," she murmured. "And Dad wouldn't have done it if I hadn't agreed to it."

"It was a life or death situation, pumpkin," Alan said, looking at Saffron pleadingly. "Do you think this is easy for me?"

Yes, she did. With the amount of money at stake, Saffron did think it was easy for her father. But guilt quickly washed over her. She knew under normal circumstances her father wouldn't willingly do what he had, right? But still, it wasn't in her nature to just go and accept things because they happened and they couldn't be changed. She was never going to be as complacent or passive as her sister.

Marigold never threw a tantrum or got upset or said a bad word. She was happy to help at any expense to herself and that's why Saffron had taken on the role of her protector or else everyone would walk all over her. Like her father was doing right now.

But she knew her sister better than she knew herself and the only joy Marigold ever experienced and was selfish about was her art. She was a stunning artist, her talent took Saffron's breath away, and now she had given it up because their father had made some selfish, stupid-ass decisions. Saffron knew without her art, Marigold could easily lapse into depression. That was never going to happen. Neither was this cockamamie deal her father had struck up to help them out of their fix.

"They were going to hurt Dad, Red. More seriously this time. But because of the deal Dad made, he's paid off Thunder Montgomery in full and we can now pay off all our other loans. It's a small price for me to pay really," Marigold said quietly, staring into her coffee. "Thunder Montgomery threatened to take us as payment for Dad's debts."

Thunder Montgomery! Let him, Saffron thought. Never had she wanted to put a bullet into a man more than the thug who was ruining their lives. Make that six bullets. One for each of his balls and two each for both his heads.

"But why Marigold, Dad? She can't handle this... this... You know that." She couldn't even bring herself to say it out loud. The whole thing was ludicrous. "Why didn't you call me instead of Marigold?"

"Because Marigold will do this quietly. And she came no questions asked. My life was at stake and if I'd called you, you would have given me a lecture first and I might have been killed. She came and she agreed to it and she was approved of, so to speak."

"Approved of?" Saffron cried. It stung a little that her father had that little faith in her. In a life or death situation, nothing would have stopped her. If nothing else, she would have gone there specifically to knock her knee into Montgomery and tell him to go and find a proper job and leave them the hell alone. "And I would have put up a fight, right, even though it was the right thing to do. To fight this. Not to just accept it. We could have come up with other solutions."

"Marigold understands how much we needed the money and I wouldn't have done this if she'd said no. What kind of a father do you think I am? I would never force my daughter to do something she doesn't want to."

"You don't even know the man you're dealing with, Dad. He could be a serial killer."

"He's very rich," her father said.

"Oh, right. That automatically makes him a saint."

Saffron threw her head back and dragged her hands through her hair. She couldn't let Marigold do this no matter how much of a knight her father thought this guy was just because he was rich. It would ruin Marigold's whole life. She was meant to be a famous artist. Marry someone who would adore the crap out of her. Someone established and smart, who knew how to take care of her and would ensure she would never have money problems. Someone who would protect her like Saffron had done her whole life.

This deal her father had made with the devil himself was not something Marigold would be able to walk away from when it was over. She would become involved, entangled, and that might lead to a lifetime of misery for her.

No. She couldn't let Marigold do this.

"You didn't ask me if I wanted to do this, Dad. So, it's unfair. You and Mom were all about being fair when it came to the two of us. I want to do this."

"Saffron," her father sighed.

"Is Marigold's name specifically written on that deal you made with him?"

"No, not really," her father answered. "But—"

"Then it doesn't matter which Sinclair daughter he gets, does it?" They might be sisters, but maybe what her father meant was Marigold didn't have pitch-black hair streaked with red, and tattoos on her ankles and wrists plus the ones her father didn't know about on the rest of her body. Marigold didn't have multiple ear piercings, or wear rings on all her fingers and two of her toes. Marigold didn't wear tattered jeans and thigh-high boots, or short plaid skirts. Her mother always said Marigold was Gold—subtle and serene. And Saffron was Red—fiery and unapologetic. Their mother had said they were perfect shades together even if they were complete opposites in looks and personalities.

"So, fair is fair. We'll settle this the way we settle everything. Toss a coin." Saffron could take Marigold's place. Her life was going nowhere very slowly and she had nothing to lose, and at least she had the emotional strength to see this through and come out of it just fine.

"Red, no. I'll do this. I'm okay, really."

"Then let's just toss the coin and see what happens. You know what we always say—"

"If it's going to happen it will happen," Marigold finished. "But you always win," she added.

"Fair is fair. Get a coin."

"Red."

"Gold."

Marigold got up from her seat and found a coin in an old cookie jar. Saffron did what she always did when they played this game and she needed to win. She put her hand behind her back and crossed her fingers. She had to win this time. Her sister's life depended on it.

"Tails," Marigold said. She always chose first. She flipped the coin, caught it and placed it over the back of her hand. She slowly lifted her other hand.

Heads.

When relief washed over Marigold's face for a mere split second, Saffron knew she had made the right choice by insisting on the coin toss and then winning the game. Her sister was not cut out for this. Neither was Saffron, but she wasn't one to go down meekly. The devil their father made the deal with had no idea who he was going to be dealing with when she arrived.

Marigold hugged her tightly. "Let's do it again. Please," she pleaded. It was just like her sister to push aside her true feelings and suffer through the things she hated. Well, that was over now.

"No way." She pulled back from Marigold but still held on to her arms. "You are going back to school now that we have this money. And you are going to be a famous artist one day soon. Me, I'm going to clean up the last of Dad's messes and everything will be okay." She wiped Marigold's tears and hugged her again then set her aside.

"And, Dad, I don't care what you do with the rest of the money. I really don't because I'm done with all this crap from you, but one million dollars goes to Marigold and you can't touch it. I think it's time you grew up, Dad. You have to take responsibility and you will soon have a clean slate to do it."

Saffron's guilt rose a notch at her digs at her father. She loved him more than her life and she had forgiven him the instant he came clean about his gambling problem and the financial disaster he had sucked them into. He was still mourning the loss of their mother. But this cycle had to stop.

Still, she threw her arms around her father, who was still seated at the kitchen table.

"I'm sorry, Dad. I know it's been hard." She kissed the side of his forehead and he held on to her arms wrapped around him.

"I love you, Red." She couldn't mistake the tears in his voice. "I'm sorry. I'm sorry for being such a loser."

"Oh, you're no loser," Saffron piped, giving him another smooch before she poured herself a glass of juice. "I have to say, you're a genius. Well, except for the part where you picked the wrong daughter, but for the rest, you are a genius. You singlehandedly now sold the *right* daughter off for a whopping three million dollars. We get to pay off stupid Montgomery, pay the banks, and this house becomes ours forever and we get to send Gold back to that fancy art school, and you'll still have enough left over for a fancy retirement. We're sorted for life. I'll say cheers to that."

Saffron didn't want any of the money. She really didn't need any for herself anyway.

She took a long sip of the juice. Now that she had saved her sister from god knew what, it would be up to her to finish the task. Suddenly a bundle of nerves settled in her tummy even though she put on a brave face and false bravado.

Marigold helped her pack quickly. Her father had made arrangements for Marigold to be picked up, probably in a limo, for all Saffron knew. And since Saffron had thwarted whatever plans had been made already, she decided to drive up there herself, a whole day earlier.

This was all happening very fast and Saffron was grateful for that, or she might do something totally uncharacteristic and break down in tears. She was, in reality, even less prepared and worse equipped than Marigold if she were really honest with herself. But there was no turning back.

Within an hour she was bundled up into her I'm-on-my-death-bed car, her bags in the back seat and a lump in her throat as she waved goodbye to her family. She refused to cry. This was only going to be temporary, if she had any say in the matter. She had all the confidence in the world she would be making the return journey back home within days and they'd be three million bucks richer and without a single problem. As long as her father stayed in check. She might have said she was writing him off, but she'd never do that for real.

She just had to play this game right.

Using her phone's GPS and still getting lost, after two extra hours of driving around in circles, she finally embarked on the longest ass driveway to have ever been invented to what was a ridiculously massive house right on the mountain. It was like a cozy cabin on steroids. She whimpered as she clutched her steering wheel, her car groaning as it made its way up toward the house. The place was practically in the middle of the goddamn forest. No other life existed for acres and acres. All before her was private land. An entire forest for a backyard. Oh, fuck!

What kind of a criminal was this guy? And he was a criminal, or he wouldn't have been at Montgomery's tables gambling, and he certainly wouldn't pay an old man for his twenty-one-year-old daughter. God help her. The only thing keeping her going was the thought that this could have been Marigold.

Chewing bubble gum nervously, she finally came to a stop—or rather her car huffed and puffed and said *no fucking farther*. She got out of the car, pulled her sunglasses onto her head and whistled. The house was just plain ludicrous. No one in their right mind needed that much space, like, ever.

Suddenly everything got that much more real. Oh boy.

The massive door opened. If there weren't any cameras around the property, then certainly the sound of her rust bucket car alerted anyone who was home of her arrival. A man stepped out of the door, drying his hands on a towel. All six-feet-plus of him eyed her with a look of suspicion. His eyebrows drew together as he scrutinized her. She waved carelessly as if to say *Okay, hi, Mr. Suspicious, you don't bother me at all. Look all you like.*

"Yoo-hoo. I'm looking for Carter Blake? You him?" she shouted from the bottom of what could only be described as a flight of stairs leading to a pyramid—aka the mansion on the mountain.

The man stood with his hands on his hips, the towel dangling from his fingers as he continued to stare at her. Okay then. Stunned, much? Unperturbed, Saffron opened her passenger door and hurled out her bags—just two, she wasn't planning on staying for too long—then made the journey up those stairs. Heaven help her, her sides were aching by the time she got half-way up. Her bags weren't even that heavy but she wasn't an exercise fanatic.

When she looked up, intent on sarcastically yelling she was fine hauling her bags up the demon-borne stairs, two other men had joined her welcoming party.

They all looked at her like she was a freak crawling up the stairs. And so they stood; one still with his hands on his hips, the suspicion in his eyes even more pronounced now that he had a close up view of her, another with his arms folded in a definite no-nonsense way while the third one stroked his jaw.

They were all massive. All about the same height, over six-foot and all super muscular. They looked like lumberjacks in their flannel checked shirts and jeans. Only, like the house behind, they looked larger than life, god-like even. Everything seemed so magnified to her. She wondered which one of them was Carter Blake and who the hell the other two were.

Dying of thirst—okay maybe that was an exaggeration, but she was very thirsty—she conquered the stairs and arrived at their feet. Oh hell, up close, they were freaking gorgeous. All three so different and yet she couldn't decide who was sexiest, the most stunning.

She dropped her bags at her feet, about three steps below them, and wiped her forehead. Even though there was a definite chill in the air because winter was around the corner, she felt hot and sweaty and breathless. The panic that had been roiling inside her all the way over here, increased and filled her entire body. She worried she might puke all over their expensive shoes and their stone-tiled floor.

How on earth was she going to do this? She barely knew her way around sex. She had done it only once before even though everyone thought she was an expert. Okay, she gave off that impression because it went her with character and her style and it meant she could be someone else and not herself.

And that one time when she did have sex, it had been horrendous. So horrendous. Her boyfriend, a sexy popular football player, had been hot and heavy for her—only to penetrate her one second and pull out and flee the next. She never heard from him again. He left town.

Now she was left thinking there was something wrong with her. And wondering if she was a virgin or not. How fucked-up, right?

And here she was. Sold for sex.

She might have thought Marigold didn't have the emotional stamina to go through the whole crazy thing, but Marigold did have a steady boyfriend—she'd had two, actually, in total—and really she had more sex than Saffron led everyone to believe she herself did. God help her. She had to keep the reason for this endeavor in mind: her father's safety and him hopefully getting his life on track; Marigold going back to school, her future taken care of; her mother's beloved house never threatened with foreclosure ever again. Basically, a cushy future for her family. She just had to make sure this here didn't last too long.

"Who are you?" The guy stroking his jaw observed her with curious intent, his brows, which looked soft and yet manly, settling in the center of his forehead as he frowned at her.

"Me? Why, I'm Saffron." She held out her hand. Not one of them took it. "You know, Alan Sinclair's daughter? I'm your baby-maker, the one you paid my father a cool three million dollars for? Now, which one of you guys is going to be my baby's daddy?"

# CHAPTER 2

*S*affron forced herself not to choke as she uttered the words. They had to know she was brazen and gave no shits at all from the start. They had to believe her tough girl act if she had any chance of pulling this off.

She folded her arms over her chest, which pushed her ample boobs together until they spilled over her tank top, batted her eyelids, and smiled as she chewed her gum. The taste had gone out of her strawberry-flavored gum an hour ago and now it tasted like pliable cardboard. Great.

But yes. That was the deal her father had made. Apparently the thug, Thunder Montgomery, had called in his debt and her father, taken with the gambling fever again, had foolishly believed he could beat him at a poker match and cover the whole debt once and for all. They'd been in that crummy shady casino where everyone knew high stake illegal poker matches were played by real criminals and they were organized by Montgomery himself.

But of course, her father lost—his bad luck had not changed one iota—and so increased his overall debt to Montgomery by another twenty-thousand dollars. *Oh, Dad.* Which was exactly how and where Montgomery wanted him. He threatened to break off his fingers with the ultimatum: pay up, or pay up with both your daughters. But then maybe her father's luck had changed after all, even if the actual price to be paid wasn't so bloody great.

The commotion Montgomery had caused in the dark dingy place where these illegal games were held had alerted one of the players who was playing his own poker match. According to her father this billionaire-cum-crime boss had come to his rescue and offered him a deal of a lifetime. A new beginning, and all it entailed was one little thing. A baby.

Was she even hearing herself think these thoughts? How did this happen to her family? And which sick bastard would offer three million dollars to impregnate and then set free the lucky, or unlucky, recipient? People with too much money on their hands. And so, voila. Here she was.

Not one of the men in front of her said a word and their scrutiny made her feel very uncomfortable. She wore blood-red streaks in her hair and blood-red lipstick, and all her piercings and tattoos and provocative clothes so that people would take one look at her and then look quickly away again. She lived for that. She lived for that instant of shock so she could be left alone the rest of the time afterward.

"Well? Cat eat your tongue or something? Which one of you paid for my body?" She tried so hard not to blush saying that—a flushed face didn't go with her demeanor—but they were so fucking gorgeous, all three of them, that they intimidated her. Made her feel self-conscious, as if they could see she hid her un-sexiness by trying to appear sexy.

"Do I have the wrong house or something?" She swirled around and all she could see were the tops of thousands of trees. She could very well be on another planet.

"You're not the girl we bought," the one with the light brown hair cut short in a serious I-don't-kid-around fashion said. He tightened his arms which were crossed over his chest.

"Oh, my god, it talks," she said, exaggerating her glee.

"Girl's got a mouth on her," the one stroking his stubble-covered jaw said, grinning at her. His hair was almost as dark as hers and shaved on the sides. His too-blue eyes drifted down her body as if he had every right to look at her that way. Perv. "I can think of enough ways to get her all prim and proper."

"Yeah, well, she's not the girl we saw. That girl was blonde, and definitely more demure," no-nonsense guy with the folded arms added. So maybe he was the one who was meant to put a baby inside her. Good luck with that, buddy. The last guy who got between her legs didn't stay long enough to do anything, and this one planned to get her pregnant? Yeah, right. She must have some guy deterrent between her legs. Oh, he was going to be in for a surprise.

"Look. I have a sister; she couldn't make it. And if you take away my hair, tattoos, and piercings, I could practically be her twin. That get you off? Fine. I'll do it. But I'm the daughter who's here right now and ready to get this baby making session going, as you paid for. I'm here, I presented myself, but if you find you can't, er, do me, hasta la vista, baby. Your loss and I'll just be back on my way." She turned around, sighing at the downhill climb but happy it went better than she'd ever expected. Game over.

"Then you won't mind refunding the three million dollars?"

Fuck. She turned around slowly. Mr. Suspicious himself had asked that question.

"No can do, mister. A deal is a deal. I came all ready and willing and you refused me. Not my fault. That's how the cookie crumbles, as they say." She turned back around.

*Please just let me go. Please just let me go. Please just let me go.*

"You'll stay," Mr. No-nonsense's serious voice boomed from behind her.

*Kill me now.*

But she continued walking as if she hadn't heard him. She increased her pace, fearing she might stumble to her death, but she was so close to her car.

"Bring her in." She heard the command given even though it was issued calmly and softly. Before she could take her next breath, her bags were taken from her and she was scooped up and tossed over one wide and hard shoulder.

What the hell!

"Put me down, you imbecile," she yelled at Stroking-jaw guy as he carried her up the stairs. She kicked and screamed and banged her fists on his back.

"You can scream all you want, princess, no one will hear you out here." The sinister threat evoked a hundred feelings in her. First, a kind of fear which transformed and settled between her legs, contracting her core and heating her skin. Okay, really? She had some sort of fetish thing going on for being helpless? When exactly did that start? She renewed her efforts and banged on his back harder.

"Stop that, or I'll slap this pretty ass that's so close to my face right now." His words just seemed to pile everything between her thighs. Was this how a mental breakdown happened? No way, and not to her.

She continued to hit him with her fists as hard as she could. Then everything happened really fast, even though it seemed to drag out second by slow second. She didn't expect the sharp slap to her ass. Tossed over his shoulder that way, her skirt was flipped up and his hand landed square on her panty-clad backside. She was beyond shocked now.

He carried her into the house and down a long, warm passage and turned into a room where he lowered her feet onto carpet so thick she sank. Outraged that Stroking-jaw guy had spanked her, she raised her hand, ready to slap the crap out of him. But she made no contact whatsoever. He caught her hand and within the blink of an eye, twisted her arm around and clasped it behind her. Her back now pulled into his hard chest. Her body had gone into overdrive.

"Never that, princess. In fact, that's going to cost you a whole lot of spanking once we're done talking."

"Screw you, asshole."

"That too," he warned. "You can only have a dirty mouth if it's filled with cock, understood?"

"Ugh. Double screw you then," she said, looking at him stubbornly. She wished she knew who she was going to be doing the naughty with. She supposed it could be any one of the three of them. No one had answered her when she asked for Carter Blake. Maybe Carter Blake was No-nonsense guy who was now seated behind a massive desk. If so, she had no dealings with Mr. Suspicion and even less with Stroking-jaw guy, who touched her as if he owned her.

"Sit, Ms. Sinclair, and if you can't do that, I will restrain you to the chair with my belt."

What a bunch of superior dicks. *Restrain you to the chair with my belt.*

Fuck him, too.

She slammed herself into the chair and crossed her legs. Her short skirt did a piss-poor job of covering her thighs and suddenly she felt tiny sitting down with two of them leaning their backsides against the edge of either side of the desk and the other seated on the other side of it, like some kind of king.

They were all so beautiful to look at, though—that thought kept interrupting her normal thinking. She didn't know who to look at the most and her gaze kept going from one end of the desk to the other. And now that she was seated, and her legs clasped together, she was certain her panties had gotten wet in between the time she was tossed over one wide shoulder then threatened with a spanking, and told to sit or she'd be bound if she didn't.

But she pacified herself. Under normal circumstances, if she saw them on any other innocent occasion, she would feel that rush of lust for each of them and she would probably go home and lie in her bed and touch herself and make herself come thinking about any one of them being the one touching her.

Then the guilt and shame would follow her quiet orgasm.

Something was wrong with her. No boy wanted her, certainly no man. And these three males in front of her were all men in the purest, most base sense of the word. One literally carried her over his shoulder and, because he was without a club, he spanked her with his hand—so, same thing, they were quintessentially men from a cave.

She swung her leg back and forth, impatient to get this over with, whatever *this* entailed. And yes, she would deal with it. She would have to do whatever it took to make sure they didn't demand their money back. Oh, god, maybe she should have played this differently. Been as demure as Marigold. Too late now. They'd spanked her and threatened her and ordered her about, she had to bare her fangs now. No one ever walked all over her. Certainly not these three buffoons.

"Ms. Sinclair, are you familiar with the terms we had with your father?"

"Yes. One of you paid him to get me pregnant. I'm assuming it's you?"

"No, we paid him for your sister."

"Well, you got me." She shook her head and swung her leg harder. "Don't like me? Then please return me. But no refunds allowed."

Stroking-jaw thought she was funny as heck. He laughed then said, "Oh, we like you just fine, princess."

Saffron rolled her eyes. Idiot.

"Unless you find you no longer want to be here, in which case you may gladly refund us our money and we'll part ways. It's very easy." Mr. Suspicious was all about her returning the money and leaving, wasn't he? His mistrust was so evident, she already felt guilty for no discernable reason at all.

Saffron stared him down but he was the first to look away. He dragged his hand through his thick wavy hair, still looking down. When he did look at her he did so as if he were worried she would steal the silverware. He looked to be uncomfortable around her.

Maybe shy even. Shy? Men were not shy around her. They either thought she was easy, or a threat.

She couldn't understand Mr. Suspicious's reaction to her, but whenever she looked at him, he looked away. Although she more than felt his gaze on her when she wasn't looking at him. Odd. He didn't seem to have the casual confidence of No-nonsense guy and Stroking-jaw guy.

She was screwed. "I'm not giving the money back. Now let's get on with this," she spoke directly to No-nonsense guy. "The quicker we get on with it, the quicker we part ways, right?" She swallowed her fear and reminded herself she didn't need to actually be sexy for him. He'd paid for her—well, Marigold, but same thing. If he—whichever of the three he was—couldn't bring himself to finish the job, that would be her perfect excuse to up and leave. She'd come—not technically. Okay, she arrived, he tried and it failed. Babies made, zero. Money kept: three million dollars.

Maybe her un-sexiness was what would save her and then she'd be free to see her father be happy and not stressed and live the life he was meant to live, and see her sister achieve her dreams. That would be all Saffron would need to make her happy. For herself she wanted nothing. Well, she didn't know what she wanted for herself and she couldn't go after what she wanted if she didn't know what she wanted.

"But humor us a little. We want to know how it is that you're sitting here and not your sister," No-nonsense said.

"So, you were expecting someone beautiful and got me instead?"

"That's not what I meant. Just tell me why you came in your sister's place. Whose idea was that? Because when we met your sister, she agreed and we made all the arrangements to get her here. We were supposed to pick her up tomorrow."

"Yeah, I know. Again, you got me, a day early. Surprise. Look, my sister is pure and sweet and a brilliant artist and she has her whole life ahead of her and I will not stand by while my father and you ruin it for her."

"Then it was your idea to come in her place?" Mr. Suspicious asked without looking at her.

"You bet."

"Your idea to deceive us, princess?" Stroking-jaw said.

"Correct. What are you going to do about it? Again, if you don't like the way I look, let me go, but that would be your problem, not mine, and I will not be giving you the money back. Got it?"

"Oh, we *got* it, all right," Stroking-jaw said, and smiled. "But we kinda just don't like deception in general."

"Too bad. I'm not saying sorry." She rose from her chair. "Look, you leave my sister out of this or I swear I'll, I'll... Just leave her out of this, okay? And since you clearly don't approve of me, kiss this," she said, turned around and flashed them her cotton panties, the ones with *fuck you* printed on her ass. She righted herself to face them.

"Look at the brat on this girl. God damn, I fucking love this girl," Stroking-jaw guy said and laughed. "I want to take her over my knee. And then my cock."

She rolled her eyes at Stroking-jaw then looked at No-nonsense guy. No-nonsense guy sat back in his chair, his hazel eyes penetrating her, and at once she felt stripped—naked and absolutely certain the other two men in the room were looking at her that way, too.

"Sit back down, Ms. Sinclair. We're keeping you," No-nonsense guy informed her. Why she obeyed she'd never know. And oh crap, they were keeping her? Holy hell.

"I think we should introduce ourselves first," he continued. "I'm Carter Blake." No-nonsense guy *was* Carter Blake. He was the one after all.

"Jack Hallson." Mr. Suspicious was Jack Hallson. He really did have the most beautiful eyes, but he never looked at her long enough for her to see the true depth of the gray.

"Caleb Jeffries, at your service, princess." Stroking-jaw aka idiot aka Caleb Jeffries.

"Well, nice meeting you all," Saffron said, she wiggled her fingers at them all.

"And you're Saffron, am I right?" Carter asked.

"Saffron Sinclair," she said.

"Now as far as you know you're here to have a baby for me, right?"

"Yup, that's what my father told me."

"Have you heard of BHJ Timber?"

"Who hasn't?"

"We're BHJ. Blake, Hallson, and Jeffries."

"Okay." She frowned. "Thanks for the back-story, but what's that got to do with me?"

"A lot," Jack said. "I don't think you fully understand exactly what we paid your father for. In fact, I'm beginning to wonder if maybe he misunderstood us too, innocently or deliberately." He rubbed his neck as he spoke and did everything to avoid looking at her.

"No. I think he understood everything perfectly fine. You paid him three million dollars to get his daughter pregnant. Nothing complicated about that."

"Let's tell you a story about how BHJ Timber started," Caleb said.

"If you must. I bore easily though, so don't be offended if I fall asleep."

Caleb laughed. "You're just adding on the spankings, aren't you, princess?" What was it with this guy and spanking? "What do you say, men, a definite attitude adjustment is required, right?" Caleb said to them all. "I, for one, am going to enjoy reddening that sexy ass of hers."

"Just try," she warned darkly. "Are you going to tell me this story or what? I'm already bored with all this talk."

"Jack, Caleb, and I," Carter began, "we grew up in a foster home. We were placed there because... Well, our parents were not very good people. We got shuffled around a lot, but we stuck together and finally found a home with a lumberjack and his wife. We were between the ages of fifteen to seventeen by then. He taught us about trees and the business of felling. Eventually we started working with him."

"So you're really lumberjacks?" She laughed. Great cover-up for being criminals. Although she had to admit they certainly looked the part. Masculine power just oozed off them in loads.

"Our foster dad forced us off to study though," Carter continued. His deep voice had a comforting timbre but Saffron couldn't deny that a level below that tone he was stern and dominant and really and truly took no nonsense from anyone. "Jack's a qualified doctor. He works on site now in case we have medical emergencies. Caleb's an engineer, he has a very high IQ, and I have an MBA."

Wow. They weren't all just brawn. So, they were smart criminals.

"And we still work on the trees right alongside the men who work for us to this day," Jack offered.

"And you still get to be villains and crime lords in your spare time? Cool story."

"We aren't crime lords, princess, if that's what you really think. Just because we play dangerous poker games with dangerous people in shady establishments means we like the thrill of danger but not the lifestyle. We have the balls to be totally legit."

"Legit? Umm... you basically paid for a sex slave to impregnate. Only the completely totally fucking psychotically insane and the criminal-minded would do that."

"I'm going to have to do something with that mouth of yours, Ms. Sinclair," Carter said darkly. She swallowed and suddenly the real threat of being punished surfaced. She quickly slid her gaze to Jack and Caleb. They weren't smiling or laughing at her either. They were pretty serious in a sexually predatory we-will-whip-your-ass-girl-if-you-step-out-of-the-lines-we-set-for-you kind of way. She remained quiet, desperately trying to stop the wetness gathering between her legs.

"We formed our own company, BHJ Timber. We're worldwide, but here's where we prefer to stay. We lived right here on this land in a tiny two-bedroom house with our foster parents and here's where we'll continue to live out our lives," Caleb said. His voice had taken on a serious tone, too, and she saw emotion in his devil-may-care blue eyes.

"We've reached the point in our lives where we've been thinking about what legacy we're going to leave behind. Life is short. But we built this company and we have no one to leave it to." It was Carter who filled her in on this part of their history.

"Okay. I see," she said. She got that part. Carter needed an heir, hence she was sitting in his chair to provide said heir.

"No, I don't think you do see exactly what we're trying to get at," Jack warned.

"I'm not stupid," she said, full of defense.

"No, you're not, but this is an unusual situation," Caleb said.

"The thing is, we're never going to marry. That won't change. Ever." The promise in Carter's voice ensured that he meant what he said.

"Me neither, just so you know." She uncrossed her leg and then re-crossed it.

"But we have this company we would like to leave to someone," Jack said.

"Someone who is born as result of us being together," Carter said. "No matter who his or her true biological father will be. That will never be questioned. Not as long as we're alive, that is." He rose from his seat then leaned against the desk, flanked now by Jack and Caleb.

Saffron resisted the urge to slide a little lower into the chair. The amount of sheer maleness around her seemed to penetrate her skin and left her trying to catch her suddenly heavy breath. Without her explicit permission, her gaze dipped to their groins. What was she doing?

Three thick bulges faced her. She swallowed and whipped her

gaze back up to encompass three sets of eyes, looking down at her. The air became too hot and scorched her body. She was going to hyperventilate. She squeaked. She sat up straighter, clutching the edge of either side of the chair until her knuckles turned white.

She knew what was coming. She knew what they were going to say. She wasn't equipped for this. She was going to die from sensory overload.

Oh, Dad, do you know what you really got your daughter into?

But she told herself to calm down. Maybe she still had it wrong. Surely. They couldn't be serious. They were messing with her because of her bratty mouth and attitude and now they were having one on her. They were going to say *kidding* any minute now. But how could her panties be getting wetter from this utterly crazy assumption? Was there something in the air messing with her mind —and her body?

And what was wrong with her if she passed all semblance of logic and went straight to the most bizarre, the most mind-stopping, the most amazing and the scariest? Surely their words didn't mean *that*.

# CHAPTER 3

*S*affron forced a huge gulp of air down her windpipe. For a moment there, she had lost it. Totally. Was she really picturing all three of them penetrating her and leaving their sperm behind in her so she could give them a baby? *What?*

No. Never. She was not mad. She had common sense even if she didn't possess a great intellect. Her common sense told her hell no, times a zillion. She couldn't handle one guy having sex with her, she was not sticking around to find out how badly she would fail three of them, all at once. No, thank you.

"You guys are," she rose from her chair and dragged her finger across the three of them, "the three of you are batshit crazy if you think that's going to happen. I didn't sign up for an orgy. Thank you very much."

"You didn't sign up for anything. Your father did," Carter said. Hell, how serious was this guy, did he ever smile? Him with his MBA and all business-like manner and everything.

"And you told my father this? You told him the three of you wanted to… wanted to…" She was getting messed up all over again.

"We made it perfectly clear."

"He spoke to all three of us, princess."

"Yes, I know, but he knew only one of you would be the one. Well, if my father had actually understood what you wanted, he would never have taken your money. Maybe you tricked him. Maybe you were ambiguous?"

"No. We left no room for any misunderstandings," Jack said.

"We all three were there. Your father knew he was giving you or, well, your sister, to the three of us. We explained all that to him very clearly and in easy terms. We are BHJ—the three of us—and that's who paid him three million dollars. A million for each of us." Carter's words ruined any last hope that they'd tricked her father. How had her father left out the part where there was going to be one of her and three of them? Had he done that deliberately? Even Marigold had assumed it would only be with one of them, she didn't know which one, she had said as much.

"You're lying," Saffron whispered although the sound of her voice echoed in defeat around the room. Something deep inside her said yes, her father could do something like this. She would have to be the last person on earth to admit he wasn't the overly protective kind, but she had come to admit it eventually. After their mother died, his daughters were more a hindrance than a help. But still, would he do this? Yes, yes, he would. For three million dollars. He would.

Saffron groaned. Her father had definitely left out two of the guys in the deal because there'd be no way Marigold or she would have agreed. He had known what he was doing. And between Montgomery and the trio making up BHJ, he'd chosen the lesser of the devils. God, was she ever so screwed. Three ways, actually. And still she wanted to believe her father wouldn't have done this. Surely not *this*.

She crossed her arms over her chest and her boobs threatened to spill forth again. Ordinarily she wouldn't care; *here, take an eyefull, you won't ever be touching them.* But this time she uncrossed her arms quickly. Something was completely out of whack with her. She didn't want them to see her flaws. Not now that she knew she would have to sleep with all three of them. Now, why would she care about them that way anyway?

"We paid your father a sum of money for you to have our baby." Jack's quiet voice played down her nerves and increased the heat in her blood.

"And by our, we mean mine, Jack's, and Carter's."

Caleb's voice flooded her cells. She couldn't breathe. She was turned on and scared, and the two feelings together were the most peculiar she had ever had in all her life.

"You're going to have our baby." Caleb's voice dropped to a dangerous level. Was she still standing or had she melted?

The things they said made her look at each of them. Her spine tingled and she wanted to bite her lip. They were so incredibly good-looking, any girl would go crazy for them. But all together? How many girls would run for the hills at that proposition? Yet the sensations inside her tripled. Okay, what in the world was happening to her?

She started backward toward the door. She was going to faint, or take off all her clothes. Carter and Caleb followed her. Jack remained half-seated on the desk. They were overly exquisite men, powerful and sexy and strong and not afraid of her, and two of them now converged upon her slowly as she moved back toward the door.

"If you're uncomfortable, we can rescind our offer and end our association." Carter's voice, soft and seductive, cut into her thoughts. Ending their association meant giving their money back then returning to her old life; one in which Montgomery would remain a dangerous, possibly fatal threat. She shuddered to think what would happen to Marigold if he got his hands on her.

Her butt bumped into the shut door. Without taking her eyes off all three of them, she fumbled behind her for the knob. But then Caleb placed his palm on the door, stopping her from opening it and trapping her between them. She wasn't going anywhere any time soon. Actually, she really didn't have any major life plans if she were honest. She was used to doing odd jobs and just hoping her sister and father were happy and content. She didn't have any big dreams, not like Marigold. Truth be told, she didn't know who she was, what she wanted to be or what she wanted from life generally. But maybe this was it. Maybe giving her sister the life she wanted was all Saffron could do. And if it entailed this, then she was okay with it.

They were so close to her, she could feel the heat streaming off their bodies and enveloping her.

"Will you let us take you that way, Saffron?" Jack said, so softly, she almost didn't hear him from the desk. She whipped her head to look into his eyes. For a brief moment, he let her gaze upon him, let the silvery grayness of his eyes slide over her. But while Carter and Caleb were sex on sticks and oozed male confidence, and it appeared as if they had the balls to seduce her into it if they chose, Jack seemed uncertain. No, it was as if he fully expected her to give them their money back and bolt. Did he want her to leave?

That insight lasted but seconds.

"Will you let us fuck you that way, Saffron? Will you let us slide our cocks into your pussy..." Carter weakened her.

"And take our cum deep inside you, from our three cocks, and make a baby for us, Saffron?" Caleb's sexy voice unhinged her.

Their voices became one, yet she picked out the nuances that made them each individual. She stood perfectly still, afraid the slightest movement would set off an orgasm. Without even touching herself. What was that? Like some mental, spiritual orgasmic experience. Was that even possible?

But immediately her age-old fear surfaced and killed the glorious though never-before-experienced feelings happening between her legs. Now there was a chance all three of them would get to reject her the instant they put their big cocks inside her. All three of them.

Because that was just how she was made. But suddenly she

didn't want them to know just how sad she would feel when they found out how undesirable she really was.

She swallowed and bit her lip, hating that she was quivering like some damn virgin. They could never see her as weak and vulnerable. She wasn't that kind of girl. She wasn't feeble and complacent for anyone. She hid well behind her bluster.

"I don't think you three can handle me, but sure, go right ahead and—"

"Spit," Carter said, holding his palm out for her bubble-gum.

What? No! It was her safety net. She stalled.

"Spit, or I'll belt it out of you."

She spat the gray gum onto his hand. She had never felt more embarrassed in all her life. Or turned on at the thought of being controlled right down to base level. But to cover up her confusing feelings and reactions, she opened her mouth to send out the retort of a lifetime and stopped the instant Carter spoke again. Somehow, in the little time she had known him, he had wired her brain to quiet down when he spoke. As if she were to hang on to his every word. God help her. Since when did she start behaving like a hormonal teenage girl?

"A few ground rules, Saffron," Carter said. With the two of them facing her now, she seemed to have shrunk in size and power. She took comfort from the door behind her, it prevented her from tipping over flat on her ass. They were all over her personal space and couldn't care that she had hung up her favorite *do not pass* sign in neon lights on her forehead.

"First, we need your consent that we're allowed to fuck you."

What? Umm, wasn't that the whole idea of them paying for it? That she didn't have a choice? "You paid for it, you can just take it."

"We will. But we prefer to have your consent all the same," Carter said. "If you don't consent to us fucking you, we'll end our dealings."

That was code for *give the money back*.

"Fine."

"Say it."

She sighed. "I consent to you—"

"Say our names, Saffron," Jack interrupted her.

"I consent that Carter and Caleb and Jack can do whatever it takes to put a baby inside me. There. Happy?"

"Thank you," Carter said.

"Now you need a safeword," Caleb said. "Do you know what a safeword is, princess?"

"A word that will stop you doing what you're doing. Why would I need a safeword? I already consented to, uh, to being with you." She swallowed. "All three of you."

"It will be a word you can use if you don't like something we're doing to you and it can apply to anything. We'll stop immediately and have a conversation about it. Understood?" Caleb lifted her chin and smiled at her.

"Yes."

"Good. Your safeword is choke. Choker is actually a logging term. So, when you use the word choke, we'll stop, okay?"

"What will you do that I might have to use that safeword?" A streak of fear ripped down her spine. What were they going to do to her?

"Among other things, we'll be spanking you when you misbehave. We don't tolerate disobedience," Carter continued. "If we tell you to do something, no matter what it is, you do it. Or you get spanked. Put your life in danger, you get spanked. Real hard. That's non-negotiable—until you become pregnant, that is, then we'll find other methods to punish your disobedience. Again, your body is ours," he said. "If we want, we can use any toys on you we like, tie you up, gag you, dress you the way we want. Or leave you naked if we choose. We're pretty isolated here, your body is ours solely and no one else will get to see you or touch you while you belong to us.

"We will most definitely be experimenting on every part of your body. Rest assured your pleasure is something we take very seriously, unless we're spanking you for misbehavior, that is. Then your pleasure might be delayed or completely canceled out for however long we choose."

Caleb took over from Carter and delivered more ground rules. "And just so we're absolutely clear; your ass? We own your ass too, princess. That means every fuckable hole you have, we'll be taking. And in case you aren't clear on what that means, we can and will most definitely be fucking your ass with our fingers and cocks and whatever else we choose, just as we would your sweet little pussy and your sassy mouth." Caleb stroked his jaw as his gaze slid down her body.

"You will be required to follow a reasonable diet that doesn't include any alcohol at all. And an exercise regime, even if it's only walking every day. Your health will be monitored too," Carter said. "Jack's our resident doc and will be taking care of you. Any questions?"

She looked at Carter as if he had grown orange colored horns out of his ass. Any questions? That was an understatement. Normal people would not be in situations like this in the first place, with three men, because this was not normal. Nothing about any of this was normal. She should say something. Where was her quick wit? Her sarcasm? Her hell nos?

Apparently, they'd drowned in her wet underwear.

"Good," Carter said, taking her muteness—her dumbstruck muteness—to mean she was right on board with everything. "Now, take your panties off, sweetheart."

Somehow the words *panties* and *off* seemed to be the trigger she needed for her brain cells to come alive and hopefully help her come up with a great retort. "Why?" Was that the best she could do as far as a great retort was concerned? She was embarrassing herself here. Who was this person she had become in a record amount of time? And did she just almost whine the word *why*?

"We know what they say."

She really should be outraged.

"And we don't appreciate the disrespect," Carter said. "Now do as you're told, sweetheart." His deep voice eliminated any argument. She hated being told what to do. Just hated it. "Or would you prefer we hold you down and take them off you ourselves?"

Good lord. The image took hold in her mind and refused to leave her. She couldn't let them touch her. She didn't feel strong enough. The strange neediness between her legs could very well strip her of all common sense and when that happened, well, she didn't want to stick around to see how crazy desperate she might become.

Giving them a look so full of attitude she risked cracking her face, she shoved her panties down her legs, turning bright red when she realized just how well the cotton had soaked up her arousal.

Without thinking, she picked them up from her feet and flung them at Caleb. He caught them with a grin on his face.

"If you think that's the last of my *disrespect*, well, there's a lot more where that came from," she said, crossing her arms over her chest, a big smile on her face. But they weren't paying any attention to her. Carter and Caleb were examining her panties. Her wetness. And now she dripped onto her thighs, so red-faced she thought flames might rise from her cheeks. Why were they doing this to her?

Their gazes locked with hers, Jack's included. She gulped down her breath. A delicious fear worked itself up her spine. She felt afraid of them. Afraid she would lose all her sense of independence if they touched her. And there'd be no going back. She had lost her marbles completely. This line of thinking didn't make Saffron Sinclair, Saffron Sinclair. Then why were these thoughts flying through her head right now?

The tension in the air spiked. The silence threatened to drive her crazy.

"We'll start in a couple of hours. You need to rest for a bit." Carter broke the tension but then took it way over the top with his words. "Caleb will show you to the room you'll be resting in. Be assured this will be the only time you will be alone. After we're done for the day, each day, we all will be sharing the same bed. Get a proper rest. You are going to need it."

"Can I have my underwear back?" The fact that her panties lingered out there in the open—okay, Caleb had put them into his pocket, but still—continued to make her feel so shy and embarrassed. Two qualities she had thought she was devoid of completely.

Caleb took her panties out of his pocket. "This pretty, wet little thing? Nah, you're not going to need any of these." He tossed her panties onto the coffee table. Good god, who were these men?

"Come on, princess, let's get you rested."

And just like that she was dismissed.

～

CARTER BLAKE'S blood roared with the familiar stirrings of lust under his skin and he knew his best friends felt the same way. Only this time, it felt different. Very different.

"Wow," Caleb said, arriving back from showing Saffron to the room where she was meant to take a nap and eat something. "Can you believe this? Fuck, she's gorgeous." He poured them all a drink.

None of them had expected her; this Saffron Sinclair with her ebony hair threaded with streaks of fire, her piercings, her tattoos, her attire. Certainly not her attitude, which they would relish readjusting.

The moment they held her panties in their hands, that innocent bikini cut cotton, hardly the kind meant for seduction, and felt its wetness, they knew they had the right woman. Their words had turned her on and they hadn't even touched her. Those weren't subtle words either. They weren't the kind of conventional words used when you wanted to get into a woman's pants. They made their intentions clear. Of course, she knew the end result would be a baby in her belly, but they'd added rules and warnings and threats.

They'd promised to fuck her any way they wanted, in every hole, until they put a baby inside her. They'd threatened to spank her, discipline her when she misbehaved, and this was how she reacted. A panty-full of sweet silky wetness.

If those things hadn't turned her on, she would have fled. And if she stayed because of the money, then why was she so aroused she had soaked her panties? They'd bombarded her with their dominance. And she'd blossomed under it.

Carter's cock ached now and he was in tune enough with his friends to know they felt the same way.

They had seen and passed hellos with Saffron's father on a few occasions at Montgomery's joint. They all knew he was a man asking for trouble and when they were there, they looked out for him. They had also seen Marigold a few times when she came to pick him up after a day of bad losses. His friends had commented that she would make a good candidate as the woman to bear their child. In fact, they had been thinking about approaching her personally and making their proposition. They were prepared to pay her any sum of money she demanded since theirs would always be an unusual request. But fate had made it happen sooner than they thought.

Not only did they save the old man from Montgomery's violence, but they gave him a cool three million dollars too, with a promise to never harm Marigold in any way.

They had looked at it as a clinical task. Sure, Marigold was beautiful. She came across as an appropriate candidate for them. She was intelligent, very docile, well-disciplined. She wouldn't give them a hard time at all. The sex would be done purposefully, with the end result always in sight. Her monthly schedule would be monitored closely and the guys would only sleep with her when she was ready to fall pregnant. Not one of them had any lustful feelings for her at all. Still, they weren't cruel. Their intention was to make the time she spent with them as comfortable as possible.

They didn't need to have their lustful feelings stirred. This was all about making a baby.

Some would say her gene pool was marred. Just look at her father—a gambler with no will to live, if they were to judge by the way he was pissing his life away. But if that were true, if Marigold's genes were marred, then his, Caleb's, and Jack's gene pools were horrendous. Their DNA had spawned druggies, prostitutes, even murderers. Yet the three of them had turned out okay. It didn't matter where they came from; it mattered only what defined them. A motto they adhered to their entire lives.

But this woman who dared to deceive them, dared to come in her sister's place and basically tell them to deal with it, well, she was something else altogether. Her sassy attitude appealed hopelessly and awoke their dominance. Saffron Sinclair could very well be their dream girl. Which was a pity since they'd vowed never to love a woman long ago when they were in their teens. That pledge had become a part of their lives. They'd never broken it, even though they had enjoyed countless women together. Not one of the three of them had lost his heart. They were too well-programmed for that ever to happen.

Now all they wanted was one woman who would take them inside her body and give them a child, an heir. The offspring born of the union was all they needed or wanted. Who the biological father would be didn't matter at all. The child would be a part of them all—no matter what. A part of the three of them. It wasn't an ordinary pact to make, sure. But they weren't ordinary individuals and they never did abide by what was right and wrong according to the norm. They answered to no one. Money brought with it all kinds of power.

Carter glanced at Caleb. A year younger than him, Caleb was the most easygoing guy on the planet, which was in direct contrast to what his childhood had entailed. Nothing got to him. He worked as hard as his high IQ demanded and played even harder. He could tell Caleb could barely wait to start on her because for all of Caleb's brazenness, it had been a very long time since he had come across a woman he wanted to chase. The same could apply to Carter, too. But Jack?

Carter's gaze next landed on Jack. He had taken a seat, twirling his drink in his hand, then he leaned forward and picked her panties up from the coffee table where they had been left. Two years younger than Carter's thirty-two, and one year younger than Caleb's thirty-one, Jack would always be considered their little brother. Of the three of them, Jack had had it the worst with his loser parents before he was taken away from them.

Carter went to Jack and squeezed his shoulder. "You okay there, bud?"

"Yeah," Jack said but Carter knew what was going through his mind. No matter how many times he and Caleb told Jack it didn't matter in the least, and fuck everyone, when it came to having a woman between them, Jack's past always remained a dark shadow for him. "It's not like she has to fall in love with us in order to have our baby, right?" Jack took a sip of his drink and then another. Saffron Sinclair evoked strong feelings in him. Jack had never allowed himself to be so affected by a woman before and his friends could see that clearly.

"Damn straight. Hey, she's crazy hot, not going to lie," Caleb said. "And her attitude, goddammit, I feel like I can be hard for days just thinking about disciplining her. Haven't felt that for a woman in forever. We all feel that way, right? We want to take her over our knees, spank that ass of hers red and make her come all over us. But the bottom line is this, we paid her to have our kid. That's the service she's giving us.

"She's taken the money, and that's what she signed up for. We didn't say we want to marry her. We didn't say we want her to fall in love with us. We bought her body, Jack, to use, to put a baby inside her—our kid—and I'll be fucked if that's going to make you feel bad about yourself, bud."

Carter couldn't have said it better himself. No matter how

alluring Saffron was, this wasn't a romance between the four of them. This was a job with a specific goal in mind. Sure, Saffron was going to make the game a lot of fun, but once they got their money's worth—a baby—they would not be sleeping with her, certainly not for any pleasure. That was not the deal they'd made. She was welcome to stay and be a mother to their child if she so desired. Or she was welcome to leave, whether she ever came back for good, or came back occasionally to visit them, the choice would be hers. But there wasn't going to be a sexual future for them after the child was born, nor one with any kind of emotional attachment.

Neither he, nor Jack, nor Caleb, would be falling in love with her. They weren't rigged that way. They may have learned to control their darkness, the one which lurked beneath the surface because of their pasts, but they all suffered from a severe case of not trusting a woman to stay. Especially a woman they loved. Their mothers had continuously chosen everything else over them. They weren't going to give another woman a chance to trample all over their hearts again.

They weren't helpless kids anymore. Money gave them power. They answered to no one but each other. And they weren't looking for the picket fence, happy ending with a woman, having lots of their babies together.

# CHAPTER 4

*S*affron had not expected to fall asleep, not with the way her body resembled a bundle of nerves. But she'd been instructed, cautioned, warned—whatever other word there was for being told what to do—to rest. She needed to be well rested for what lay ahead.

She had so many things going through her mind, a zillion things, and she couldn't get a handle on them all. Three lumberjacks. A baby. Punishments and spankings. Panty thieves.

Maybe she had met with an accident and knocked her head and was having this bizarre dream from her hospital bed. But she never bullshitted herself. This was as real as fuck. These lumberjacks would punish her with spankings and they would get her pregnant and once the baby was born, they would send her back on her way. On the surface, it wasn't much of a big deal. Surrogacy was a huge thing these days, and it helped couples have babies if they couldn't on their own. But the operative word there was *couples*. One man. One woman. One surrogate. Not three men, one woman.

But who was she to judge? She may kick up a storm for it being unconventional, but she hardly had the right to judge them. She knew what it felt like to be judged. She was judged every day, all day long for her fashion sense. But this was personal. She would star as the main character. This was happening to her.

It would feel as if she were kidnapped by aliens, three to be precise, who probed her a few times then kept her for nine months before they deposited her back on earth after she delivered their baby. What had she really gotten herself into? And worse, she still hadn't come up with a solution. The thought of leaving was still first and foremost on her mind. Not because she was sanctimonious about the whole idea, but because she didn't trust herself around them. Yet...

The truth was if she walked she had to give the money back. If she wanted to keep the money for her family, she would need to have their baby. A baby they wanted to be a part of all three of them. Obviously only one of them would truly get her pregnant, but as they had said, they wouldn't be finding out who the lucky sperm donor was. Was that like a ménage pregnancy? Was that even a thing? But better her than Marigold, which remained the only incentive she needed to take on the world which in this case happened to be three rich lumberjacks.

She lay under the covers, snug and cozy, staring at the ceiling. It felt odd to nap in the middle of the afternoon. The nerves in her body buzzed uncontrollably and the heaviness between her legs made its presence known with every breath she took. What witchery had she gotten herself into, and why was this affecting her body the way it was?

Eventually she did fall asleep, maybe for half an hour, and now a weak sun began disappearing from the large floor to ceiling windows. She sat up and glanced around the room. A tray graced the table and the aromas made her tummy growl. When had that gotten in? But she was starving and didn't question anything except what to eat first. She gobbled up cheese and fresh fruit and a perfect chicken salad. She ate a muffin and drank juice and tea. Satisfied and energized, she moved on to her next task as instructed. Sleep until you wake then eat. A shower was meant to follow her eating.

So that's what she did. She couldn't help but be enthralled by the sheer luxury of her surroundings. These men certainly lived in style. Everything was top notch quality and looked imported from some European country. Not that she was usually impressed with materialistic things.

After her shower, she was meant to put on a gown. Were they going to, uh, do her now? This early in the evening? She stepped out of the shower and wrapped herself in a thick fluffy towel. She sniffed at the jars of lotions lined up on the vanity and skipped her regular brand which she'd brought with her and tried one of theirs, clearly bought specifically for her. She couldn't imagine them using lavender or rose scented anything on their persons. They were way too leather-and-wood rugged for that.

Caleb had told her to come down in only the gown and nothing else. She wouldn't be herself if she didn't defy him, so she rummaged through her bags and found the perfect pair of blue cotton undies. She frowned at the word—it didn't quite work—but a bright idea exploded in her head. She found one of the markers she usually carried around in her handbag and corrected the print.

Satisfied, she slipped them on and put the gown on. The silk glided over her skin. What were those lotions made of? They were bound to cost more than she made waitressing in three months.

She might as well get started on it. No use prolonging the inevitable. Which could turn out perfect for her. Once they saw her completely naked they might run the same way her one and only boyfriend had run. There was always that hope.

She made her way carefully down the stairs, not being able to stop herself from admiring the house. There was a nice warmth to it and the windows were positioned perfectly so that the late winter sun warmed the rooms during the day. The furniture was classic male—wood and leather but inviting and comforting.

She trailed her hand down the paneling alongside the staircase. Someone had carved that by hand. Very talented. But which one of the three of them did that? Probably Jack. He came off as reserved, quiet. He hardly said anything to her at all, and he wore that suspicious look each time he looked at her. That kind of art work required traits of the personality he had shown her. Definitely not Caleb. The man preferred no-holds barred flirting as his pastime. He didn't have the patience to sit down and work with wood that way. Definitely not him. Maybe Carter? No, it was Jack. Definitely Jack.

She landed on the bottom step and stood still. She had no idea which way to go. But before long, Jack approached her. He wore a white doctor's coat over his jeans and shirt and her heart missed every other beat for several seconds. There could never be a sexier doctor alive.

"Saffron," he murmured.

"Hi," she said, all bright smiles to camouflage her nervousness.

"Follow me." His softly delivered command resonated as nothing but curt with her. Maybe he really didn't like her at all. She said nothing further and followed him to the other end of house.

He opened a door. She stepped inside and nearly tripped over backwards. The room before her was an honest to goodness doctor's room. Steel cabinets lined one wall, a cold and clinical steel table stood at the other end, with more cabinets on that wall. There were a desk and laptop, a patient's bed, stethoscopes, and a scale, and a blood pressure machine, and some other doctor thingies she couldn't name. There was also a full lounge area on the other side. She swallowed as her gaze went over to one of the tables gracing the center of the room under a startling fluorescent light.

Her body hadn't told her mind why it was suddenly so hot under the silk gown. She turned to face Jack.

"This way." Jack gestured toward the scale. He still refused to make eye contact with her and she couldn't understand what she had done to him to warrant that reaction. Okay then. She stepped out of her sandals and stepped onto the scale. She didn't bother looking down. She was not ruled by her weight. Yet that Jack would know this little intimate detail about her sparked a flush in her cheeks.

He took a seat behind the laptop on the desk after making her sit in a chair opposite him. "I need some information before I can continue with your exam." He fired up his laptop and asked her a list of clinical questions about her health and her family's medical history. Her mom had died in a car crash she hadn't caused and her father was still as fit as a fiddle even though he was a gambling addict.

Jack still never once looked at her as he questioned her. She desperately wanted to tell him to go to hell. But a part of her was more intrigued by this man than anything else. It bothered her, as if she were missing a puzzle piece. She knew where to slot in Carter and Caleb, but without much from Jack, the image remained incomplete. She thought of them as an inseparable trio already. But what was his beef with her exactly?

"You don't like me very much, do you?"

"I don't need to like you."

"No, you just have to screw me. Your share in the three million dollars' worth, I get it. I bet you'd want to do it with the lights off. Or would you prefer I wear a brown bag over my head?" she asked, spreading her lips into a sweet smile. Why did it bother her so much that he didn't like her? Why couldn't she get over it already? This wasn't going to be some soppy romance thing for any of them.

"Your task is solely to have our baby. I don't need to like you for that to happen."

"But how will you bring yourself to—" She hesitated. She swore very well and never thought much about it. But she never used the F word to actually mean sex. She tried again, determined to treat him as coldly as he treated her. "But how will you bring yourself to fuck me if you can't stand the sight of me?"

He paused to consider her, then looked away again. "Perhaps I will use the brown bag after all. Now, can we continue? Are you a virgin?"

And just like that he doused her spirit and took her back to that night when her boyfriend of six months had left mid-coitus. How many girls could say that? Now how did she answer that question of his? She wasn't quite sure. At her silence, he lifted his head and glanced at her.

She whipped her gaze down. "No," she said. Next, he asked her about the state of her sexual health, did she have this or that STD. She answered no to everything. She was secretly celibate but they didn't need to know that. He asked about her period and she wished the leather in the chair would open up and swallow her whole.

"What happens if I don't fall pregnant? If I can't?" She had not thought of that before.

"If it's a medical reason as to why you are unable to conceive, then we will part ways." He paused like he always seemed to do and gazed fleetingly at her. "You'll keep the money in that case," he added. She blushed because that was what she was thinking.

But then he asked about the state of her orgasms, and she almost forgot to breathe. No problem there, she rushed to say. She could orgasm, she just felt a little sad whenever she did. He was making it very hard for her to maintain that tough girl act with the blatant questions and words and warnings.

He took some blood for tests and showed her all three of their medical histories which showed they were squeaky clean. He then told her to stand.

"This will be cold," he warned as he placed his stethoscope on her chest. He merely moved it under her gown, listening intently to her heart beat. Satisfied, he removed the stethoscope at the same moment that Carter and Caleb came into the room.

"Why hello again, princess."

She glared at Caleb. What were they doing here? Why did her

temperature spike to all sorts of crazy highs? The three of them in one room had a potent effect on her body.

"Are you well rested?" Carter asked her.

He put his hand on her shoulder which seemed to dissolve all her clever comebacks to his question. She answered with a soft yes, instead. *Kill me now.*

"Good. Then let's get on with it," Carter said.

Jack rose from his seat. "Remove your gown please."

Saffron shot up from her seat. Oh my god! Was it really going to happen here? "Why?" she cried.

"I need to examine you. Now please remove your gown and get up here." He pointed to medical chair in the center of the room.

"Fuck no. I'm perfectly fine. You don't have any reason to examine me. And I'm certainly not going to let you examine me in front of them. That's just crazy and not right and—" She might have to pass out to calm herself. But god, no. What perversions awaited her?

"Your first rule is doing as you're told, the instant you are told," Carter said.

"Well, your rules are wrong, buster. This is crazy."

"For your disobedience, you will now be strapped to the chair. Get on there right now and you may save yourself a whipping and a ball gag," Carter continued.

"I… You…" She stomped her feet. "You're all sadistic pricks," she said. She wished she were more enraged, more outraged. But the only thing she experienced a hundred times over was embarrassment. Embarrassment that they would see her naked, that she would be helpless and at their mercy. Her anger was more at herself for her body practically turning into flames the way it was.

They were going to see her naked. Completely. Would they be able to tell from looking at her naked body how un-sexy she was? She wanted to cry. She had hoped against hope that when they had sex, it would be in a dark room so they couldn't see her. Now she had to strip for them and, oh hell! She'd seen the straps where her ankles would go. How high the bars were where her calves would rest. Anyone who sat in there could be spread wide. Good grief.

But at least she'd have the last say.

She turned with her back toward them and shrugged out of the gown. Then, to make sure they read the word on her panties, she bent slightly to lay her gown over a chair. Laughter resonated around the room. That was Caleb but she may have even heard Carter's brief chuckle in there somewhere. A fitting term for them. The novelty panties—she had bought a few online—said *dick*. Until she'd improvised and added an *s* with her marker so that it read *dicks*. She didn't discriminate and didn't want any of them to feel left out.

"Take your panties off, Saffron." She straightened her spine at the sound of Jack's voice issuing his command. She took a deep breath and shimmied her way out of them. There was no way she was getting on the chair without turning around and giving them a full view of the rest of her lady bits. She forced herself to think about Marigold. She was doing this for her sister.

She turned, and unable to be brave enough to walk with confidence to the chair where they all now stood, she blocked her breasts and her vagina with a hand each and, as awkward as hell, walked toward the chair.

"On all fours, please," Jack instructed.

"Are you fucking insane?" On all fours would mean her ass would be in the air.

"I need to take your temperature."

*From my ass?*

Her gaze went from Carter to Caleb to Jack. They all looked at her expectantly as if this were completely normal.

"You are all a bunch of lunatics," she grumbled. "And you two aren't even real doctors," she said to Carter and Caleb.

"Oh, we just like to play doctor." Caleb winked at her.

She huffed and got onto all fours. Hands immediately went over her behind. Cupped her, lightly spanked her. Her eyes teared as she tried so hard not to be aroused by the fact they all stood behind her scrutinizing her ass.

She could make their touches out. Jack's was the easiest. He wore gloves and she couldn't understand why that hurt her on some totally irrelevant level. Carter's big hand kneaded her. Caleb's kept parting her cheeks, but not completely. He teased her.

*Please god, don't let them see my wetness.*

"Lube," Jack said and it sounded more like a question than a statement.

"Let me," Caleb said. Of course he'd be the one to offer his help. With fingers that weren't encased in a glove, he rubbed the lube all over her anus. The freezing cold gel made her nipples ache anew. She bit down on her lip when his finger slipped inside her then out again to bring in more lube. Her whole womb quivered. Her pussy pulsed. None of those were the right reactions.

She had never, ever been touched there before. Anything anal made it to her list of no- ever-fucking-way-ever. Suffice to say not even a doctor had taken her temperature this way. But here she was with three incredibly sexy men, gritting her teeth trying not to… what, exactly? Implode? Explode? Detonate? Orgasm?

"I think I got her good, Doc," Caleb said.

Jack's one latex-covered hand rested on her lower back. "Take a deep breath. It doesn't need to go deep, but since this is your first time, just relax." As of a few minutes ago, Jack had her entire sexual history on file. Anal sex had been a no when he'd asked the question. Maybe she should have said *hell no*—that might have meant off limits since she wasn't equipped to handle this kind of sensation.

She took a breath and he inserted the end of the thermometer into her. It wasn't that big and except for the foreign intrusion, didn't hurt at all, not with the amount of lube Caleb had played into her ass.

"Keep still," Jack instructed. "It will take about a minute."

That minute turned out to be the longest in her life.

"Look at that ass. See anything lovelier?" Caleb mused.

"She had anal before, Jack?" Carter asked, to which Jack answered no.

"She's as tight as fuck, I can tell from slipping my finger inside her. It's going to take some work stretching her to fit us."

Saffron shut her eyes and prayed they wouldn't see how flushed and feverish her body had become at their words. She was so turned on, the dying need to touch her clit would soon override all common sense. They wanted to take her temperature? Well it would read *on fire*.

A sudden bleep sounded in the room and relief washed over her. Because they were going to take the thermometer out or because it meant they were going to touch her again? She didn't quite know.

Jack pulled the thermometer out. Carter's fingers slipped inside her and she basked under his grunt and softly delivered oath.

Caleb playfully slapped her ass. "Good girl," he said.

"Onto your back, please, Saffron."

Would the humiliation never end? When she was on her knees, she had managed to keep her thighs tightly closed, to conceal her wetness. On her back, with her legs spread wide—because if she knew them, that's exactly how they would want her—how could she hide her arousal? There existed practically no hope for her.

She turned around onto her back as Caleb and Carter sanitized their hands and Jack pulled on a new pair of gloves. Her legs dangled over the bottom. They would now see everything. Jack pulled a chair closer to her and raised one leg until she bent it at the knee and it rested on the bar. She closed her eyes. He had a perfect view of her vagina now. While he did the same to the other leg, Carter and Caleb restrained her arms to the chair. She was completely spread and bared and strapped down with no escape in sight.

"Fuck, she's glistening." Caleb whistled.

Carter drew his fingers down her slit. She shuddered. Her back arched at the contact. She groaned out loud as he dipped between her folds right into the copious wetness in her center.

"Look at this," he said. She opened her eyes only to catch a glimpse of Carter's hand in the air, her wetness dripping from his fingertips before she shut her eyes again. Was it even possible to be that wet? Was that normal?

"Good, healthy self-lubrication," Jack murmured as he next inserted two fingers inside her with his gloved hand. He went deeper, stroking her insides, and yet she knew he was examining her. Maybe that's what turned her on so much. She was being sexually examined by three hunks and only one of them was a real doctor. And he didn't even like her.

"Ah, look at that pretty little clit." Caleb pressed her clitoris between his thumb and forefinger. Her head came off the headrest. Her body spasmed a little at the attention on her clit and with Jack's fingers still inside her, he would feel it. He locked his gaze with hers for but a second before he removed his fingers. She could have died from embarrassment. "Everything seems to be normal."

She didn't know why she had this reaction to him. Carter and Caleb made it clear what they intended to do with her. But Jack had kept silent, except for the part where he offered her a chance to give the money back and the question he'd asked about her being able to give them what they wanted. Maybe he did look at this thing as nothing but a clinical task.

And that was how he examined her too. She could see clearly Carter and Caleb's erections and she couldn't deny the warm glow that erupted from her skin at their arousal for her. Did Jack have one under his doctor's coat? Maybe. She doubted it.

But then he looked at her again and she knew instantly the chance of him being sexually attracted to her was zero. His gaze still held some suspicion but for the rest he could have been looking at a table instead of her. Or someone with a brown bag over her head. Seriously, though, how many times did she have to tell herself this wasn't going to be a fun escapade? There would be no flowers, no champagne, no wedding ring afterward. Jack had the right idea. Now she just needed to follow his example.

Jack searched in a drawer and drew an oddly shaped item out of it. She raised her head again but with her arms bound at her sides, she couldn't get a proper look at it.

"What is that?" she squeaked.

"A speculum," Jack said as if she should know what that meant.

"A specu-what? What are you going to do with that?" She wriggled around the chair, trying to free herself.

"We're going to get a very up close and very personal look at you, sweetheart. Don't worry, it won't hurt." Carter's tone may have been comforting, but his words destroyed her. Were they going to put that inside her and then open her up?

"And if it does it will be a good hurt." Caleb added with a wicked smile.

She dropped her head back down and squeezed her eyes shut. Fresh moisture pooled in her sex and slid toward her ass. She was not going to make it, not without one hundred percent completely embarrassing herself in front of all three of them.

# CHAPTER 5

*F*ingers touched her again and her legs shook.

"Looks like she can do without the lube," Carter said even though he poured a warm oil all over her center then brushed it in.

Caleb parted her folds. "I can't wait to see inside her. Gorgeous inside and out," he murmured, stroking a single lip of her sex.

Carter held the nozzle of the bottle between her separated folds and squirted more lube into her. Saffron shut her eyes as he used his fingers to massage it into her. *Don't come. Don't come. Oh, god, just don't come. Ever.*

Jack's gloved fingers entered her next, ensuring she'd been lubricated well enough. His fingers glided over her flesh. She lifted her head to catch him drawing his brows together in full concentration mode. His calmness and professionalism were in direct contrast to the state of her aroused body.

"Relax," he said softly and penetrated her with the instrument. The cold steel brought a sense of relief to her hot sex but she warmed even the steel soon enough. As if he didn't get a good slide in the first time, Jack slipped the speculum out of her and then pushed it back in again. She tossed her head to the side and chewed on the inside of her cheek.

She couldn't come. No matter how bizarre the situation, the only person touching her right now was Jack and he was the real doctor and he didn't even like her very much. In any other ordinary circumstance with any other doctor, even thinking about an orgasm right now would have revolted her.

But here she was bound, strapped down, helpless even as the sane part of her brain screamed at her to use her safeword, or risk total humiliation by climaxing. But her lips wouldn't form the word. That easy word. But she choked. So easy to say. It would definitely apply here. They said she could use it for anything she didn't like. Her body just wouldn't allow her to say the word.

"Breathe," Jack instructed. But she held her breath as the instrument widened inside her. Slowly. Torturously slowly. Carter and Caleb stood on either side of Jack. Carter with his arms folded. Caleb stroked his jaw. Both their gazes remained fixed on her vagina—the vagina being spread apart by Jack for him and his friends to see inside.

It didn't hurt so much as embarrass her. She had gone her whole life with only a fleeting moment of attention paid to her private parts courtesy of her boyfriend, and now, within hours of meeting them, she was completely and thoroughly exposed to three sinfully gorgeous lumberjacks who wanted her to have their baby. In what world was this right that she got turned on by the position they'd placed her in? She should have been fighting, cursing, using her safeword. She should have dried up like a desert. But she did nothing of the sort. She didn't breathe, because breathing would...

"Breathe," Jack said, a little more forcefully this time as he placed his other hand on her mons. His palm accidentally—definitely accidentally—touched her clit. Immediately a breath stumbled out of her mouth and an orgasm escaped her, the same orgasm which had been pent up inside her for too long and now flooded through her.

"Did she just fucking come right now?" Caleb asked softly.

*Oh god, help me.*

"Yes," Jack said quietly.

"She's beautiful," Carter said softly, staring at her sex. They could see what she was feeling. A tumble of contractions in her inner flesh. They could see her spasming. They could see *everything*.

Why oh why did she do that? She would never look them in the eye again. She forced her muscles to tense up, for the tremor in her legs to end. She wished for her breathing to be less haphazard. For her nipples not to be so hard.

"What do you say, Doc? Everything okay?" Carter asked.

"Yes," Jack replied.

"No, keep that in her a little longer," Caleb said. He immediately took the chair Jack vacated. "She's goddamn incredible. Can't wait for us to slide our cocks into that soft hot wetness of hers. It's going to be mind-blowing."

No. No. No. She refused to let herself listen to his words. She squeezed her eyes shut so tight she wondered if she would give herself a headache. They were bad words and enticed more ache in her sex. It was all wrong.

"I'm going to examine your breasts now, Saffron."

Her eyelids jumped apart at Jack's words. He stood beside her now.

He undid the cuffs at her wrists. "Raise your arms above your head." He removed his gloves and her throat dried. This was torture. The instant he touched her, her nipples swelled to twice their size. He probably thought she was a deviant or something. That she got off being examined by a doctor. That wasn't true. She wished she could tell him that. But she'd been rendered speechless.

The whole scenario worked against her. How could she remain impartial when all three of them were here, coupled with the knowledge she was going to have sex with them—all three, at the same time. The way they watched her. The things they said. They had put her on a sex-induced roller coaster ride from the moment they made her kneel for them so they could take her temperature anally. Everything played against her. She had no hope.

She bit her lip so hard, her nerves cried out in protest. Jack touched her breast. He kneaded her, pressed into her. With her center so exposed, a wildness settled into her. She didn't care that she would start begging for their touch. Shamelessly.

She had no control as she arched her back, desperately wanting Jack to pinch her nipple. The times he accidentally touched them, it was brief. She wanted him to touch her provocatively, sexually. But he remained professional and that drove her even wilder.

She started to writhe. Her body flushed in embarrassment as it still did what it wanted to. Jack switched over to her other breast and she couldn't take it anymore. Not with Carter watching her every little movement from the inside of her. He poured his dominance over her and she wet herself even more when she glanced at his cock tenting his jeans.

Not with Caleb between her legs, her pussy stretched and exposed for his viewing pleasure. His eyes had turned dark with lustful promise. Not with Jack's hands on her breasts. Even though he remained the most unaffected, she wanted him, in her madness, to touch her unprofessionally. For him to lower his head and suck her nipple. For Carter to do the same to her other breast. For Caleb to take her clit into his mouth. She'd never had those kinds of fantasies before. What was wrong with her?

A soft moan escaped her lips as Jack bumped her swollen, achy nipple.

"She wants to come again. Don't you, princess? You want us to fuck you *right now*, don't you? You're dripping." Caleb touched her inner flesh, so lightly and so gently. "You want that, don't you, princess?"

She shook her head in denial but failed at convincing anyone.

"Is she all good, Doc?" Carter asked. The tenseness in his voice could have broken a tree in half. "We need to get on with it and take care of that pesky problem before we can fuck her."

"Yeah. She's perfect," Jack said, his gaze passing over her face and body.

She was quivering with need now. Who was this person she had turned into and so quickly?

"We get the blood results tomorrow but I don't see any problem with her falling pregnant."

"Good, let's get on with it."

Caleb rose and Jack took his seat again. He pulled on another pair of gloves. He really couldn't bear touching her, could he? He released the speculum from her. And now he'd see all the arousal dripping from her. Jack looked up at her for a split second again before he turned his attention away and started to wipe away her wetness.

Carter pulled her up from the chair and set her onto her feet. She wobbled against him and he drew her close into the hardness of his body.

"I got you. You did well, sweetheart. You're everything we want."

Immediately her gaze went to Jack who was sanitizing the crap out of his hands.

"My gown?" she asked Carter.

"You won't be needing that just yet," he replied.

Caleb handed her a bottled water and she sipped thirstily on the cool drink. What more was going to happen to her here today? What *pesky* matter had Carter been referring to? He left her standing there in the middle of the room, in her birthday suit, her body still flushed, more moisture pooled between her legs even though Jack had tried to wipe her dry. Carter took the single seater, Caleb sat on the windowsill, and Jack leaned against his desk.

Maybe it was a matter of which room she was going to sleep in that they wanted to discuss with her. It could be nothing even. Until Carter spoke and she wished he hadn't.

"Saffron," he started. "We already explained our rules. But there is the matter of your deception that needs to be handled. While we're very happy you are the one who showed up, and we do understand your protectiveness toward your sister made you do it, we feel if you could deceive us in this one thing, you could and would deceive us in other things too. So you'll have to be spanked to prevent it from happening again for whatever other reason. We just won't tolerate dishonesty.

"We take deception as a very serious offense. One spanking will not be enough to get it out of your system for good. That's why this will be the start of a series. We'll start tomorrow. We want to give you a chance to have a good night's sleep. Plus, you were amazing today with your examination and we don't want to overload you too much all at once.

"Carter will go first. I will have my chance the next night, and Jack the night after that. This will ensure you don't ever deceive us again. If you have a problem, you come to us and we sort it out. A spanking will make you remember that. Do you understand, princess?"

Carter stood. His height was intimidating. Saffron bit her lip, and swallowed her wise crack. She couldn't seem to think of a way out of it, and she could talk her way out of anything. If only her body weren't acting so strangely. And if only she weren't naked in front of these way too beautiful men, she might have found something smart to say.

Why was she going through all these sensations? And why did she suddenly feel so bad she had tricked them? Not so long ago she had said she was not sorry. And she wasn't really sorry, there was nothing she wouldn't do for Marigold. Although, they'd made it clear she wasn't going to be spanked so much for deceiving them about Marigold, but rather to ensure she never deceived them again in the future.

On top of all that, she was so wet, she feared they'd hear how wet she was if she moved. After her no-holds barred examination, she thought she would be over it. Add a spanking, and apparently it became a perpetual sense of embarrassment which turned her on. She didn't want them to know she was a freak. And she had swallowed her tongue, really, she must have because she had no smart retort to deliver. No snide comment. No nothing. Her gaze again searched for Jack. He hadn't moved. Hadn't said a word. He looked at her with shielded eyes. What had she done to him? He put the fight back in her for sure. Even if it was very little fight.

"Oh heck no. If you think I'm just going to bend over and allow you to spank me so I never deceive you again, you all can take a long walk off a very high cliff." But even she knew she was fighting a losing battle. These powerful and super arrogant men were not going to start giving in to her whims. They planned to dominate the crap out of her.

She didn't get any further than a breath. Carter charged toward her and cupped her face then crashed his lips down on hers. He sucked her breath into his mouth and forced her to part her lips and breathe into him. He kissed her like she'd never been kissed before. His tongue slid deep, his thumbs caressed her cheeks.

A hand splayed across her tummy from behind her. Caleb. He softly kissed the side of her neck and his other hand slid toward her mons where it rested there. She whimpered to think if he lowered his hand he would know she'd become wet all over again.

Even though her faculties were under such sensational attack, given the sexual onslaught she had been subjected to the moment she stepped into this room, she couldn't help but search out Jack. He remained still, leaning against the desk, watching her being kissed and handled by his two best friends. She couldn't understand why she needed to make sure she looked at him every few seconds even when she was at risk of thawing right before their eyes at Carter's and Caleb's touch.

Caleb then started to nibble and suck on the other side of her throat. He boldly ran his tongue over her flesh then bit into her. She groaned into Carter's mouth, whose kiss smoldered, nurturing the fire roaring inside her. His jutting cock sought the area between her thighs. She was so dizzy. She wasn't standing on her own two feet, but was rather held up by the two of them.

A thousand flashlights exploded inside her. Caleb's hand traveled to her breast. He thumbed the nipple which had longed to be touched ever since Jack had taken them between his hands.

Carter slid his tongue deep into her mouth then took her hand and placed it over his rock-hard cock. He inflamed her with his hardness. She groaned. He was bigger than her hand and oh so thick. Did men actually get to that size? Carter pressed her palm against him and moved it up and down. She wasn't thinking right when she wished she were touching his bare cock.

She struggled for air and Carter took pity on her and released her lips. Why was she not stopping them? This wasn't meant to be a seduction. There shouldn't be this kind of play. Certainly not turning her into a stupid slave for them a couple of hours after meeting them. But they'd paid for her. More precisely, they'd paid for her body.

"What are you doing to me?" she managed to squeak out.

"Whatever we want," Carter said and gave her to Caleb.

"We own you, princess," Caleb said and lowered his lips to hers. Heaven help her. He pulled her head back by her hair. Wasn't she just kissed senseless seconds ago? And yet she melted all over again. He teased and bit and licked before he went in for the kill. Then he lifted her onto his rigid cock and ground her against it. Her cheeks heated up because she knew she would leave her wetness on his jeans. Her core buzzed with uncanny need. Suddenly Carter enveloped her too.

"Every part of you," Carter added. "But we won't be fucking you or touching your pussy until your punishment is sorted. And we prefer to make you come when all three of us are with you. But you're hot, sweetheart. You're dripping all over us. We can't touch you but you can touch yourself. Just let your finger slip inside that hot pussy, play with your clit until you come. You need it, sweetheart."

With him at her back and Caleb still nibbling on her throat, Carter's words took her arousal to a whole other level. They wanted her to make herself come, because they couldn't, not until they'd spanked her. They were trying to help her?

No. She couldn't do that in front of them. Touching herself was a private thing.

Caleb picked up her hand and licked her fingers. Butterflies burst from her tummy. He then put her fingers in his mouth and sucked, making them completely wet.

"Touch yourself, princess. Fuck that pretty little clit you have. We know that orgasm you had on the chair isn't enough to sustain you until we can fuck you. We know you weren't prepared for that one. It happened accidentally."

"But now you can make yourself come hard, and long, and you can scream all you want. We'll catch you, sweetheart. Just fall for us." Carter pulled her harder against his rigid cock. He bit the side of her neck.

She couldn't. How could she?

Caleb brought her hand to her center. She shuddered as she made contact with her hot flesh. "Just slip them in," he coaxed. "Feel the wetness, rub it over your clit. Fuck yourself, princess, now."

His command startled her into action. Her folds parted. She moaned at the wetness gathered inside her. The amount scared her. The heat from her sex wrapped around her finger.

"Put another finger inside yourself," Carter instructed. "That's it," he encouraged her when she obeyed him. Perspiration spread over her nakedness. She leaned her head back against Carter's chest. "Three fingers, now, sweetheart. Three fingers, baby."

She turned her head and took in Jack. She looked past his unreadable expression.

"Pump them, Saffron." Carter's breath labored in her ear. She heard the arousal in his tone as if it were her own.

"Harder, pump them harder. Rub your clit, princess," Caleb said huskily. He gripped her under her knee and lifted and parted her leg, spreading her open. Her other hand snuck toward her mons and dipped over to her clit. She whimpered. The fever was too great. No common sense could be salvaged. She had both her hands down between her thighs. She touched herself just like they asked. She gave herself permission to come. Told herself that she had no choice. They owned her. They'd paid for her. They could do with her what they wanted. She had no choice, not since the moment she'd stepped onto their land.

She couldn't have stopped the climax if her life depended on it. It rushed through her and uprooted her completely. She shook and quaked and shuddered and spasmed. She tossed her head from side to side against Carter's chest and tried desperately to take her leg back from Caleb's hold. She needed to press her thighs together, afraid she would die from the pleasure this orgasm had given her.

And, just like that, she remembered the feeling she would get afterward. The sadness. The undesirability. The un-sexiness. They would see it now. She had gone and showed them everything now.

"No."

"Don't stop. You're fucking beautiful, Saffron. You're sublime, ethereal. Fuck, you're just incredible," Caleb said, letting the last specks of her orgasm leave her before he lowered her leg to the floor and sweetly kissed her lips.

"Just lovely. You're ours," Carter said, husky and possessive. He turned her around to face him, then gently ran his thumb over her swollen lips. "Our beauty. Our woman."

The sadness that was meant to have hit her already seemed to have disappeared. The only feeling floating around her head was one of contentment. What? Contentment? Not satisfaction, but just a feeling that everything was going to be okay.

"Come on, let's get you to bed, princess. You have a spanking day tomorrow," Caleb said softly. He scooped her up and carried her out of the room and after a few minutes, he laid her down on the bed a size she had never seen before. He tucked her in, politely told her no when she asked for her pajamas, and then slid in beside her until she was forced to lay her head on his chest. She didn't think she could sleep that way. Caleb, Jack, and Carter still remained complete and utter strangers to her—but she fell asleep almost instantly.

Her last thought was about tomorrow. Tomorrow she would replace her spunk and attitude and come out all guns blazing. She wasn't going to be all submissive and passive and do whatever they said. That wasn't her. Today they'd caught her off guard completely.

They were going to get what they wanted, obviously, since she wasn't giving the money back at all, but she didn't have to go down meekly. She then drifted into that blissful place called sleep.

Her dreams were momentarily interrupted when she was pulled into Carter's side. How odd that she knew his feel, his scent, already.

But no Jack. She stirred at the subconscious thought.

Why, though? What did he have against her?

# CHAPTER 6

*F*inding herself alone in that gigantic bed, Saffron rose gingerly. Where were they? She found a flannel shirt on a chair and put it on. It worked as a dress as well. She padded her way downstairs, trying not to make too much noise in case she alerted them of her presence.

She still wasn't sure how she was going to behave around them after yesterday. She'd met them, been told she was to be with all three of them, and was examined thoroughly—although that gave new meaning to the word examined. She was spread open, forgot herself and accidentally had an orgasm and then when asked to touch herself to have a better orgasm, well, she'd done that too, no hassle. Heat blossomed on her cheeks. That must have been another person doing all those things. It couldn't have been her.

Craving a glass of juice, her equivalent of coffee, she made her way to the kitchen. The silence stretched throughout the whole big house. Perhaps they'd gone out already. They said they worked every day, maybe they were out felling trees by now. She breathed a sigh of relief. At least she would have time to gather her wits.

Clearly, luck had overlooked her this morning.

There they were, standing around the kitchen, drinking coffee from manly mugs in front of plates heaped so high with food they created breakfast mountains. She should have put proper clothes on.

"Good morning, sweetheart," Carter said. He flipped an egg then came toward her. Her heart stopped beating. The day after and they were all even more gorgeous. She had no business being here with them. She was still as un-sexy as she was yesterday and all the years before that.

He planted a kiss on her forehead. "Sleep well?"

"Yes, thank you," she replied.

Caleb took her from Carter and nuzzled her neck. "You smell so fucking good this time of the morning, princess." He released her then gestured toward a coffee mug.

"No, thanks, just juice," she said and immediately her gaze went to Jack who'd been in the process of filling his glass with orange juice. He paused for a split-second, filled the glass then handed it to her. *Well, good morning to you too, Mr. Sour-pants.*

"Thank you, Jack," she said, adding sparkle to her voice. She was not going to let him get to her.

"Sit," Carter ordered. Caleb pulled out a chair for her and she sat. Carter then placed a plate in front of her which included everything from eggs and sausages to grilled tomatoes. He also set down a fruit smoothie next to her plate. "All organic. All highly nutritious food. We want a super healthy baby. Eat up."

Her stomach growled and she gave in to it immediately and started eating. When they said they worked alongside their men felling trees, they took that seriously. They were dressed like typical lumberjacks again. Jeans, heavy boots, flannel checked shirts. But they certainly weren't ordinary lumberjacks. She couldn't get over how tall, strong, rugged, intense, and just utterly magnificent they were.

"A few things before we leave. You aren't allowed to make yourself come," Carter began. She almost choked on her sausage. "We took pity on you yesterday, but that was also just to prepare you for

61

this. Until your punishment has been delivered, you will not be given or be allowed any climaxes.

"Understand, princess? No fucking your gorgeous pussy with your fingers, no rubbing that pretty clit on the arm rests of our furniture or our pillows either. No coming means no coming. We'll be home a little later in the evening today, but when we return you will be waiting, kneeling on the floor in Doc's rooms, naked for Carter's spanking. Make sure you've eaten already by the time we get home. Mary-Ann will prepare you something for lunch and dinner. You'll need the sustenance." Her eyes widened involuntarily and Caleb laughed. "Yes, princess, it's going to hurt real hard and real bad. Now do you understand?"

Her heart beat crazily. The nerves in her butt pulled taut. She had never been spanked before. She should get all high and mighty about it right now. Chuck her plate at them and tell them to spank themselves. But that would prove futile. They would spank her anyway and add more whips for her disobedience. As she glanced at them, a single truth hit her full in the center of her being. She couldn't afford to be in their company a moment longer than necessary. She needed to get on with it, get pregnant and then leave.

She would take her spankings and get them over with without putting up a fight or crying too much if it hurt. Oh, god, it was going to hurt, wasn't it? She glanced at their hands. Big, strong hands that could turn her butt into a red ball of flames in seconds. How was she not going to cry?

"Mary-Ann and her daughter will be here shortly," Caleb added.

"Mary-Ann is our housekeeper, by the way, and her daughter helps her out. She comes by three times a week," Carter supplied her with more information. He then bent and kissed her head.

"Until tonight, sweetheart, when your ass is all mine," he whispered. She shivered at his words. Caleb kissed her next, winked at her then left. Jack barely looked in her direction even as he dished out a series of vitamins into a tiny little glass for her.

"Take these," he said and left.

An odd sudden coldness enveloped her when she was left on her own. How much space had they taken up in her life already that she wasn't sure what to do on her own? After finishing her breakfast, she downed the vitamins then took her smoothie with her and went in search of the shower. But Mary-Ann and her daughter, Lou-Ann, arrived before she made it to the bedroom. She apologized for her choice in clothes and explained she was about to change. They waved it aside and said they knew who she was and were very friendly and enthusiastic and offered her their help with anything if she needed it.

Saffron excused herself and took an extra-long shower, letting the powerful jets hit her body in all the right places. Her mind drifted to everything they had done to her and her pussy throbbed. She could so easily make herself come. Who would know? Certainly not them. But she couldn't bring herself to do it. She really needed to have her head examined, pronto.

She wasn't much of a social butterfly, she was polite, but truth be told she really liked the two Anns on first sight very much, and went in search of them after her shower. While Mary-Ann waited for the laundry to be done, and Lou-Ann vacuumed, she pulled out her knitting from a basket and finished a sweater she was making for her grandson.

"Do you knit?" Mary-Ann asked her.

"Oh, no. I can't even sew. But it seems interesting." Saffron liked to watch the way the patterns formed. It reminded of her being a child and watching her mother knit. She'd always been mesmerized by it.

"I tell you what. I'm finished with this sweater now so I'll leave this basket here for you. You can try if you want. And I'll show you when I come by again, if you'd like."

"Thank you," Saffron said and couldn't help the swell of emotion inside her. Mary-Ann reminded her so much of her mother.

"You're here to make them happy. They deserve it, those boys," she said, her eyes fogging over even as she smiled warmly at Saffron. Saffron blushed. How much did the older woman know about their arrangement? Did she know Saffron was going to have one baby for the three of them? But that was the deal. They'd paid Saffron to do a job for them—have their baby. They weren't looking for a wife. And, really, she wasn't looking for a husband either. Certainly not husbands, for sure.

After a while she left the Anns to their work and wandered around the house. The bedroom she had slept in last night was obviously her room and the guys would be sharing the room with her. They had their own rooms too and she soon drifted to them. Jack's was a medley of neat and messy. Kind of like clean clutter. Caleb's, good grief. It looked as if a tornado had visited his room and had loads of fun. If she had to start cleaning it, she wouldn't know where to begin. She smiled because somehow it was just like Caleb and his high IQ.

She walked into Carter's room next. Whoa. It was almost a shrine. Did he even use this room? Everything was in its place, not even a speck of fluff could be found. She wondered if she should remove her shoes before stepping in. She opened a couple of drawers and lo and behold, color-coded frigging everything looked back at her. He went beyond neat freak; he was certifiable.

*...your ass is mine...*

His words from this morning popped into her head. She narrowed her eyes then smiled as an idea came to her. A perfect, very effective way to get back at him for the spanking he planned to give her tonight. And so she began. She opened every drawer in his room and ruffled it up. She mixed his socks with different pairs, then put the mismatched pairs with his boxer briefs, then put the whole mess in the drawer meant for toiletries. She messed up his closet; took shirts off of the hangers and dropped them onto the floor.

Satisfied she had disrupted every single drawer and closet in his room, she tackled his bathroom next. She imagined him putting his toothbrush just exactly so every morning and moved it the other end of the counter. She couldn't hold her laughter in anymore and gave in. He was going to be so mad when he discovered this. *Well, that's what you get when you mess with me.*

When she finally walked out of the room, nothing looked as if it had been changed. But inside the closets and drawers existed enough mayhem to send a neat freak into a proper craze. She dusted her hands. Her job was done.

She spent the rest of the day reading a book she took from their rather extensive library. She lunched with the two Anns and even napped for a little bit. The two Anns left soon afterward. She'd be lying if she said at every point in her day she hadn't been thinking about touching herself and that the thought kept her in a state of wetness all day long.

The later it got, the more her nerves started to go crazy. *It was going to hurt. It was going to hurt.* Punishments are meant to hurt. And Carter was so big.

When she could delay no longer, she showered again, hoping to relax her frazzled state. She softened and scented her skin with more of the potions she found and slipped into her gown. She contemplated putting on a pair of undies with an appropriate word on them for Carter, but decided against it. Instead she picked one that said *asshole* and put it into the pocket of her gown. She would not go down without a fight.

She went to Jack's docto room and the swell between her legs doubled. Was this going to be the room where they'd torment her? And by torment she meant make her so wet and so crazy with lust she would do anything they asked. No, she rectified. This was the room where they would get their money's worth and she would just have to go along because she didn't have a choice in the matter. Saying that made her feel better about her reaction to them.

She removed the gown, took the panties from the pocket and kneeled. God help her. Her nipples were already painfully erect and she'd created fresh moisture between her thighs. She kept glancing at that forsaken chair where she'd been spread mercilessly for them the day before.

For a fleeting desperate moment, she wondered if she should just make herself come. This heaviness inside her messed with her thinking. Again, for some insane reason, she obeyed them and instead squeezed her thighs shut.

She didn't know how long she waited like that and remained in that state of deep almost hypnotic arousal. Where were all these feelings coming from, and what were the words to describe them? She was the least sexy person to have ever walked the planet and now she was like this? Because of three guys who didn't care for her modesty one bit? They were domineering, commanding, and said embarrassing sexual things to her at every turn. That turned her button to 'on' apparently.

She held her breath. Footsteps sounded in her ear. She didn't know what to do, get hotter and wetter, get up and hide, or just start begging straight away, telling them that she'd learned her lesson and she would never deceive them ever again for as long as she lived.

She bit her lip. Oh crap. She'd never been into the whole lip biting thing, not until she stepped into their house, and now she bit her lip left, right, and center. She whimpered aloud. Her skin sizzled. Oh, boy. They were coming for her.

Carter entered first. Caleb followed him. Jack was nowhere to be seen. She really needed to train herself better against his obvious rejection of her, so it didn't hurt as much as it did. But she couldn't and his absence stung a lot.

They had showered—the scent of freshly showered male enveloped her—and they were now dressed in comfortable-looking track pants and t-shirts. She lowered her eyelids when her body soared in appreciation of their amazing good looks. A shyness settled in her, too. They slowed their pace when they entered the room and now stood looking down at her from their massive heights. Her whole body warmed and must have been a pretty shade of pink. She was naked and they could see her breasts. She fought the strongest urge of all her life to cover her breasts since their gazes lingered on her erect nipples for longer than she could stand.

She didn't need to be told she pleased them. She could feel it in their presence alone, the sound of their breathing.

"Perfect," Carter said. "Are you ready, sweetheart?" She opened her mouth to speak, and it wasn't going to be anything pleasant but then Carter waved his finger at her, stopping her. "Just a 'yes, sir' will do."

*Fuck sticks.*

"Yes, Sir," she whispered. Caleb's chuckle poked at her and she raised her head and stuck her tongue out at him since her hands were held behind her back and tightly clutching her panties and she couldn't use the middle finger. He laughed even more.

"What's that in your hand," Carter asked once he'd circled her.

"A present for you, *Sir*," she said, so coy she wanted to throw up on herself.

"A present? Well, let me see what it is."

She handed him the ball of fabric. He opened up her panties the right way because the word *asshole* was right under his nose. He gave her a severe look, although his jaw twitched as if he were suppressing a smile.

She smiled sweetly and lowered her gaze again. "You're welcome, Sir."

"She's asking for it, isn't she?" Caleb said.

"I think she'll now have to give me a proper thank you after I spank her ass all shades of red," Carter murmured and tossed Caleb her panties. *No!* She was never going to get them back now if Caleb had them.

Carter then took a seat on the sofa. "Crawl to me, sweetheart," he instructed. Her heart had a mini explosion. "Now, Saffron."

She went onto all fours, fully aware that Carter would see her breasts swaying softly and Caleb who now stood behind her would see her ass, her whole ass. Just as she neared Carter, Jack stepped into the room. The fact that he had come, somehow gave her more confidence. Even though he didn't like her for whatever reason, he still had to be a part of it. And that, weirdly and crazily and completely ludicrously, completed her.

"Good girl.' From a drawer in the small desk next to him he pulled out a funny looking object. "Do you know what this is?"

It looked like some sort of sucking thing, maybe a baby's toy. Then it dawned on her. *No way.*

Carter smiled. "It's a butt plug, sweetheart. For each of your spankings, you'll get a butt plug which will get bigger and bigger. This is to stretch you and since you've never had anal sex before this will also serve as extra punishment. But the end result will be to stretch your virgin asshole until it can take a cock. Understand?"

Her eyes may have bulged. Her pulse beat wildly but she couldn't say anything to contradict him.

Not waiting for her to come up with a reply, he continued. "Now lie over my lap." Carter patted his thigh. That thick masculine thigh which could crack tree trunks. Why did she have to be so wet already? What was wrong with her?

She rose and immediately decided to get this over with quickly. She lay down, her belly positioned on the hardness of his thighs.

"Hands on the armrest." He sat in the center of the huge sofa and she had to stretch her arms to reach the armrests. "Keep them there. Move them and that's an extra two strikes. You remember your safeword?"

She nodded, all other words escaped her.

"Good. Now just relax. This will hurt, sweetheart." And on that note his massive hand landed on her butt. She shrieked and cried out and swore viciously. She hadn't expected him to really spank her. She had hoped he would say it was a trick to try to get her reformed. But he did. He truly whipped her ass with his hand.

In her shock, she started to get up but was instantly pressed back into position. Her gaze sought out Caleb and Jack's. Carter probed her ass-checks. Lube slid into her. He was going to put the plug in now. Before she could turn her head to glare murderously at him, he'd already begun to thrust it into her. She straightened and froze, shutting her eyes tight.

"Relax, sweetheart. It's just a tiny plug." With that he pushed it fully inside her and all her focus was consumed by the plug which was in her ass. This was real. Oh, hell. Carter massaged her ass cheek.

"There. That stays in you for the night, sweetheart."

What? The whole night? She opened her eyes and sought Caleb and Jack again. They were her anchors now as Carter quickly issued a second strike, harder than the first. She acted the same way, wriggling to get away from him. Hissed and swore.

"You frigging beast," she yelled.

"Decorum, sweetheart, please, is a great turn on for me. Now what did I tell you about your hands?"

"Decorum my ass, you—" Another hard smack had her whole body jiggling.

"I decided I will continue spanking you until you learn to take this like a lady. Do you understand?"

She remained quiet. She was not going to talk to him ever. "Do you understand, Saffron?" he asked again and this time the darkness in his voice made her shiver.

"Yes, Sir," she whimpered.

"Good. Now, a lady will keep her hands on the armrests without moving them an inch. She won't say a single word. She certainly won't be cursing. It's unladylike. Now stretch out your legs. And point your toes." His hand rested on her thighs and his touch coaxed her to obey. She stretched out her legs and her toes until they were almost tucked into the end of the other side of the sofa.

"That's it, now cross your ankles."

She did as she was told.

"Ah, stunning," Carter said and delivered an evil-hard slap to her globe. She dug deep for inner strength and stayed still but she wasn't going to have any lip left by the time he was done the way she'd been biting them. Another slap followed quickly. Tears were gathering in her eyes. And her wetness was great, she could feel it under her, on his gray track-pants. He would see it when she got up.

"You're doing great, my little lady." Another punishing slap. Her flesh flamed. Was she on fire already? "Now, did you fuck yourself today, Saffron?"

"No, Sir," she answered quickly. Maybe that would lessen the punishment.

"You sure you didn't finger fuck yourself? Slide three fingers into your cunt and imagine it was the three of us fucking you, huh?"

She couldn't help it. If she moved just a little, she could use his hard muscle to come. His words were driving her insane.

"No, Sir," she almost screamed.

"That's a good little girl." He praised her, but landed another scalding whack. His hands were so big he could—and did—cover almost her whole butt. She was stinging with pain. But she wouldn't allow a tear to escape. She never cried. Not for anything.

But how could she detest this painful spanking so much and still get aroused by it? How could the two go together? She needed to come. Now. She had to or she would go mad. She started to move, rubbing her clit against him.

A succession of three slaps robbed her of her breath.

"No, sweetheart. If I let you come, how are you going to learn your lesson?"

She was whimpering softly, pathetically, and yet she didn't want this to end.

"What is your lesson, Saffron? Tell me what lesson we're trying to teach you."

"Not to... not to deceive you ever again."

"Excellent." He punctuated his word with another hot shot on her ass. "And will you?"

"No, Sir. I won't. I won't, Sir. Not ever."

"That's all we ask, sweetheart. Now let's finish this up. Repeat after me—I will never deceive my men again."

As she started to repeat the words, her attention on Jack and Caleb the whole time, Carter took his attention back to her ass and seared her even more. After three times of repeating those words and who knew how many spanks she'd taken, he finally caressed her charred ass. His touch was so gentle now when just moments ago he took great pains to teach her a lesson.

"By the time Caleb and Jack are through with you, you definitely won't deceive us again." He lifted her up and set her on her feet.

Her backside must be glowing red. Surely.

"Now, aren't you going to thank me for your lesson?"

What? Did he have no sympathy? She was burning up right in front of him, for goodness sake. "Thank you," she said begrudgingly.

"That's not the way to thank your Sir for a lesson well delivered, sweetheart."

"Thank you very much for my lesson, Sir?"

"Try harder."

What did he want from her?

"Thank you very much for my lesson, Sir which I appreciated and—" She stopped short when Caleb came toward her and whispered in her ear. Her jaw dropped open. The sizzle in her ass spread to every other part of her body. He wanted her to say *that?*

# CHAPTER 7

Saffron's gaze sought Carter's. His hazel eyes had turned a dark shade which thrilled her. She saw in his eyes that Caleb had whispered into her ear exactly what Carter wanted to hear. And now that she was given permission to think it and say it and actually do it, she had been subconsciously consumed by it since the moment they touched her.

She had never done it before. She wouldn't even know how to begin. But the need screamed at her. Carter had primed her body through her backside for this end result exactly. It might not be a big deal for other more experienced girls, but for someone who considered herself to have zero sex appeal, it was huge.

But she wanted it. So badly.

She lowered herself onto her knees in front of Carter, just as Caleb had told her. Her heart beat so fast, her whole body shook. She winced as her backside made contact with her legs. It felt as if she would never know what it would feel like not to have been spanked so thoroughly. She looked up at him.

"Please, Sir," she started, then stopped. She had to say exactly what Caleb told her to say. "Please may I suck your cock, Sir, to thank you for my punishment," she said softly.

"You may, sweetheart," Carter said and pulled down his track-pants. His cock sprang free. First, shock ran through her. He was enormous. What did she expect with his overall masculinity? His thickness and his length made her feel small and inconsequential. Like a slave to a man-god. Then desire drifted through her. She licked her lips. Her pussy ached anew.

He took himself in hand, stroking his hardness. The head glistened with precum. Her mouth watered. She had to know what he tasted like.

She leaned into him and his clean fresh soap scent filled her nostrils. She stuck out her tongue to swipe his cockhead and moaned as she got a taste of him. He tasted so good, she needed more. She reached for him, but he gripped her hair tight.

"Hands behind your back. I only want your mouth," he said, tilting her head up toward him. "Now open wide, tongue out."

She did as she was told and closed her eyes when he guided his heavy weight into her mouth and rested his cock on her tongue. He pushed in, sliding down her tongue until she thought she would gag. Saliva filled her mouth.

"Yeah," he said when she did gag. "That's how I like it, wet, sweetheart."

She opened her eyes and loved the look in his eyes. Ever darker now, they dropped closed as she started to suck on him, guided by need and not experience.

She sucked him hard, until her jaw ached a little. He pulled out of her for a few moments and played his precum along her lips. She licked her lips and opened her mouth again. Without the use of her hands, she had to use her mouth to keep him inside her.

She licked and sucked harder because he seemed to like that. He hadn't released his hand from her hair and now he pulled harshly at the roots as he fucked her mouth.

She was delirious with sexual arousal. She only wanted to please him, whatever it took. She ached to use her hands, but the forbidden use of them strengthened the erotic feelings for her.

Carter groaned long and hard. She'd been so interested in sucking him, she forgot to worry about her inexperience, her undesirability. In what seemed to have become a habit for her now, she looked for Caleb and Jack. Caleb sat with his legs wide apart. His cock tented his track-pants. She couldn't see Jack's legs from where she kneeled, but his gaze penetrated hers and even now she couldn't understand the look he was giving her, when this time she wanted it to be desire. For her. She needed this. She needed it three times over.

"I'm going to blow. This is how you thank me properly, sweetheart. Swallow everything I give you. Don't close your eyes." Carter's back arched. His cock turned even more rigid. He exploded into her mouth. Washes of soft warm waves splashed into her. She kept her gaze on him, breathing and swallowing, and even just trying not to choke made her feel like the sexiest woman alive. Eventually his squirts lessened but he let her suck him clean before he removed himself from her mouth and lifted her up into his arms. He cradled her and kissed her lips so tenderly, her jaw, too. Her whole face.

"You did perfect, sweetheart," he whispered. He carried her to their room and straight into bed. After he laid her on her tummy and rubbed a soothing oil into her still red-hot buttocks, he brought her against his chest and fed her the most delicious and decadent chocolate in the world. He had made it especially for her. When, she would never know, maybe last night when she was asleep? A treat for taking her punishment so well, he said. She fell asleep not long after, right there in his arms.

~

WHEN SHE AWOKE the next morning, Carter was still sleeping next to her, with Caleb on the other side of her. As usual Jack was not around. It was Caleb's turn tonight to teach her never to deceive them again. What would happen when it was Jack's turn? How was he going to spank her? With a ten-foot pole because he couldn't stand touching her?

She eased out of bed, careful not to wake them, and slipped on one pair of their track-pants which were way too big for her and one of their t-shirts.

She went into the kitchen and found Jack there.

"Good morning," she said, overly chirpy. He grunted something at her and poured her a glass of juice. She didn't know what to say to him. He seemed so closed off from her. What had she done to him? She sipped her juice as he mostly ignored her by reading stuff on his tablet.

Caleb entered the kitchen next and gave her a big kiss on the cheek. He helped himself to some coffee.

"Where's Carter?" Jack asked. "We have that meeting this morning."

"Big guy is still asleep." Caleb's grin said it all for him already. "Guess our little brat over here tired him out, didn't you, princess?" He stalked toward her. "Did you like it? Swallowing Carter's cum like that? What made that pussy so wet, it tried to hump my thigh last night, hmm?"

What? Oh, god, no.

"You're lying," she said red-faced and threw an apple at him. He caught it, closed in on her. "Jack saw you, too, when he came to get us up. I had to pry your soaked pussy off my thigh because you know you're not allowed to come until Jack's spanking. Plus, you left a big ol' wet spot right there on my thigh. Jack saw that too, princess. Must admit feeling your soft pussy lips rubbing up against my thigh, your hard, little clit and your wetness, made me so fucking horny. All of us, princess. We wanted to fuck you right there and then."

Maybe she should have been indignant. Outraged that he would say such an embarrassing thing to her. And that Jack had seen it, too? That—that made her forget all her humiliation and instead what did she do? She got wet all over again inside a pair of track pants belonging to one of them. She, the shameful orgasmer, was hot and bothered and wanted to come like there was no tomorrow. She wanted to come with them inside her. She had lost the plot, forsaken reality and wanted nothing more than to dwell here in this place where she was constantly aroused and they thought she was sexy. Except maybe for Jack. She still couldn't figure him out. He would be a part of the three of them when they tried to make a baby with her, but would he rather not?

"You're wet right now, aren't you, princess? You're going to squirt for us when we do let you come, aren't you?"

Her brain scrambled for a quick insulting reply which didn't work in accordance to how Caleb had reduced her to a puddle of weakness with his brazen words alone. But just as she was about to say something, the whole massive house shook as if an earthquake had struck loose.

"Saffron!" Carter bellowed from upstairs. Even the windows rattled in fear. Oh, boy. He'd discovered her little trick.

"What have you done now?" Caleb asked, suspicious, but grinning at her at the same time.

"Nothing," she said, all innocent-like. By their narrowing eyes, both Jack and Caleb didn't believe her.

In a matter of minutes, Carter came pounding into the kitchen, virtually smoking out of his ears. *Man, don't mess with his order of things, or prepare to be eaten alive.*

"You." He pointed at her, fuming mad. Saffron stopped and stood still. "You're fucking lucky I'm not taking you over my lap again and spanking more reform into you. I can't believe this. We're spanking you for one offense and you commit another."

Bravely she closed the distance between them. "Are you sure you want to spank me again? I might have to thank you again and I believe you slept like a baby because of it." She teased him. Rather she played with fire.

Clearly exasperated, he ignored her completely and spoke to the other two men in the kitchen. "We need to fuck this girl soon.

Goddamn." His grunted words made her radiate from the inside out. "There are so many spankings in your future, you might never be able to sit," he said, taking a rushed sip of his coffee.

After a quick breakfast because they were late already, Carter grabbed her and kissed her goodbye thoroughly before he subtly issued a warning for her. "You will spend the rest of the day putting my closets in the order you found them. One thing out of place, and I'm going to take a wand to your clit and just before you come I'm going to put you into a chastity belt for a week. We'll be fine, sweetheart. We can fuck your mouth to our heart's content. But you? Will you be fine? You can't hump a thigh with a chastity belt on, can you?"

Oh hell, they all knew what she did in her sleep. She wanted the tiles to part and swallow her up. With that, Carter left. Caleb's turn next.

"My turn tonight, princess. You going to be ready? I'm going to enjoy that ass so much." He rubbed his hands together and crazily enough she gasped as a phantom smack landed on her behind. She almost yelped, too. "You'll wait the same way you did for Carter, got it? Make sure you have something to eat. And don't even try playing a trick on me, princess. But just to be safe, I'm going to give you extra spanks in advance anyway." He ran his finger down her cheek and over her lips. She wanted to open her mouth and bite him. But more spanks. They were really all about obeying and discipline and all that crap. And now she'd be getting extra punishment on the off chance she went ahead and played a trick on him the way she had Carter.

She folded her arms and sulked. More so when Jack barely looked her way as he walked out of the door.

"How are you going to stand punishing me if you can't even touch me?" she yelled after him before she could stop herself.

"I'll be using my belt," he called back without turning to face her or missing his stride.

She gulped and heard it so loud in her ears. His belt. Holy cow.

She swirled around and faced the kitchen. And sulked even more. Now she had to go and right Carter's closets. That was going to take her the whole day and she really truly didn't want the chastity belt thing.

After showering, she immediately started on her task of reordering Carter's room. The two Anns weren't coming in today so she was all alone. By lunchtime she had opened every drawer and closet again to make sure she had put his things in their correct order. Basically color-coded, white to black and then gray.

Satisfied with her reparations, she climbed onto his bed, curled up and took a nap. She awoke famished some two hours later and ate some of the leftover pie Mary-Ann had prepared yesterday while she texted Marigold and checked up on her father. Tapping the fork on her plate, a plan brewed in her head. How was she going to get back at Caleb? She was definitely not going to be a good girl about it, anyway. Not this time. Her lips broke into a massive smile. She knew exactly what to do. Since Caleb seemed to have an obsession with her panties—obsession meaning he had taken away three of hers already, she knew precisely how to repay him.

Taking an apple with her, she went to her room to get all the markers in her bag and came up with three: black, pink, and purple. She then went into the laundry where Mary-Ann had left her sewing basket for Saffron to learn how to knit and sew if she wanted. Then she went to his bedroom and for a fleeting moment thought maybe straightening his room would set him off but she vetoed that. He was Caleb, he would take pleasure in messing it up again. He was such a boy.

She searched his drawers and finally found what she was looking for. And they were all white. How perfect. Gathering them all up in her arms, she went to the massive dining room, chucked them onto the table then sat.

A wicked smile played on her lips as she gazed at all his perfectly snowy-white boxer-briefs spread on the table. She laid them out properly then used her teeth to pull off the marker's lid and got to work.

She spent a very long time decorating his boxer-briefs. She drew flowers and hearts and attached bows, buttons, sequins and glitter from Mary-Ann's sewing basket. When she found a packet of tiny balls which jingled, she laughed out aloud. She would be attaching two balls on either side of the crotch to as many boxer-briefs as there were jingly balls in the pack. She wrote little sayings, too, like *I have feelings too* on one, and *I'm fragile, please be gentle* on another. She went as far as to caption others with *don't worry, my dick is bigger than my IQ.* She giggled at that one.

When she was done, she looked at the collection of boxer-briefs, once pure white and super masculine and reduced now to all that glitters with bows and pretty, pink buttons. Her pussy clenched when she imagined how mad he was going to be at her. But when she thought of her spanking tonight, the ache inside her tripled.

She glanced at the old-fashioned clock on the wall and gasped. She'd spent hours glamorizing his perfectly pristine, white manly-man undies and now she'd have to scramble to shower and get ready for when they arrived. Lucky, she had eaten enough lamb pie for both lunch and supper and the apple more than filled her up.

After she showered, and scented her body with one of those luxurious lotions, she put on her gown and skipped to the doctor's room. By the time she arrived, removed her gown and kneeled in the same position she had the night before, she was hot, heavy and very bothered. The core between her thighs livened up even more. Her nipples pebbled and all she could think about was each of them taking turns sucking them.

The same as yesterday, the sound of their approaching footsteps speeded up her breath and her body glowed anew. She had better not be getting used to his kind of evening. After Jack got to dish out his punishment, it would be over. Then they would have sex, and if her cycle was anything to go by, she'd be pregnant. She was going to have their baby.

She hadn't really let that thought sink in. She had said it a lot, but now, knowing them the way she did, their influence over her body, the idea became phenomenal and... Her train of thought stopped abruptly as they entered, Jack with them this time. She breathed a sigh of relief at seeing their faces and her heart filled with happiness. She'd never admit it to them, but she missed them. Even brooding Jack.

"Princess," Caleb murmured as he came to stand in front of her. As before they had showered before they came to her. She imagined felling trees to be a sweaty but sexy job. She'd never allowed herself to think those kind of thoughts before.

"Sir," she answered immediately without even thinking about her response.

"Are you ready?" he asked. She nodded, her gaze still downcast. "Follow me." He needn't have said on all fours since at once she started to crawl after him. Already her backside stung in anticipation. But more than that her mouth watered of its own accord. Would she need to thank Caleb the same way she'd thanked Carter?

He led her to a long leather bench.

"Up and flat on your belly," he instructed her. She bit her lip and climbed onto the bench. The leather was cool initially against her hot body, but soon it warmed under her. "Arms stretched out straight ahead of you."

She gripped the edge of the bench, her face resting on her right cheek.

"Open your legs, princess. Carter and Jack would like to see what your pussy does when I'm spanking your ass."

She was on fire now and there remained no hope of her ever cooling off. Like, ever. She spread her legs. Oh god help her. Now Carter and Jack could see everything. She tried to clench her muscles as if to hide herself, but that served only to make her want to come even more.

"Beautiful. You remember your safeword?"

"Yes, Sir," she said, her voice already hoarse with arousal.

"Good. Also remember, no rubbing your pussy on my leather, princess. You be very still, all right, while I do this." Lube filled her asshole. She braced herself. She had taken a sneak peek at the size of the plug beforehand and gulped painfully. Caleb pushed it into her at the same time as he began his onslaught on her. As if her nerves remembered what they had done when Carter spanked her, they all screamed and fled, leaving her shivering at the shockingly sound smack and the full penetration of the plug in her ass which stretched her quite hard. The burn inside and outside her ass seemed to unite in the center of her sex.

But where Carter brought his palm down on her, Caleb alternated between his four fingers and his palm. He whipped her hard, leaving her a quivering mess on the bench. The intensity became too much for her, and she started to squirm. To keep her still, Caleb swung his leg over her, facing her ass, and used his thighs to keep her in place as he bombarded her ass with smack after smack. Her legs shook. She was so aroused, she could come right that minute if he didn't stop spanking her.

He must have read her body because he then clasped a globe in each hand and stretched her open, deepening the plug in her ass and exposing her pussy for Carter and Jack. Even though he thwarted her orgasm, he made her even wetter by baring her so plainly to his friends. He squeezed her flesh hard and when she whimpered, he resumed smacking her this way and that. She was blood red already in the face and she was sure her backside looked the same. She bit back swear words and instead grunted unintelligible sounds.

"Why are you being spanked, princess?"

"I... for deceiving you, Sir," she hissed as he layered another spank into her.

"Will you deceive us again?" More whacks. More wetness. More craziness that had her feeling more empowered than ever.

"No, Sir. Never. I will never deceive you ever again, Sir. You have my word, Sir," she whispered, the words falling urgently from her mouth.

"That's a good girl. Just one more lesson from Jack and you will never break your word to us." Caleb now rubbed her cheeks. She was very sensitive and wriggled. The leather under her clit felt so good, the pressure what she needed. If only they would let her come.

"We're done, princess. Up you go," he said and helped her to her feet. He brushed her cheek with his thumb. "Are you going to thank me for your punishment?"

"Yes, Sir," she said at the same time as she kneeled down in front of him. Her butt hurt like hell, the plug felt enormous and that hurt transformed into something else entirely in her pussy. A week ago, if anyone dared to lay a finger on her, she would have kneed the person.

But here in this beautiful house, in this very room, here where she was being objectified, her body soared to life and her pulse raced and she wanted to be told what to do and how to do it. She knew that would please them. She wanted to be used by these men she had met mere days ago.

Wait? She? A closet submissive? Never ever in this lifetime. She was an alpha female. In charge. No bullshit. Never mind that they'd effortlessly stripped her of her control, never mind the helpless feeling had so turned her on, her pussy ached like it never had before. Those were just lapses in her tough girl act. And she was a tough girl, dammit.

But all she thought about was whether, after Jack, they would spank her again and again. Teach her lessons. Obedience. Take her submission as a gift from her to them. The truth was that only three men in the universe could spank her. No one else could or even would, except them.

Caleb removed his cock from his track-pants. Obediently she slipped her hands behind her back. Her lips parted as she leaned in toward him.

"Unh uh, not so fast," Caleb said stroking his enormous cock. "Look what you did to my bench, princess. You need to clean that up first."

She glanced at the bench and could have died on the spot when she noticed a big wet spot of her juices on the black leather. She had leaked her arousal while he'd spanked her. Exactly what kind of kink was she really into, though? Flushed full in the face, she started to rise, looking for a tissue or something.

"Back on your knees. You'll have to clean that with your mouth, princess."

# CHAPTER 8

$\mathcal{S}$affron's eyes may have jumped out of her head. The pure dirty decadence in Caleb's command skyrocketed her arousal. She searched for Carter and Jack's faces. Carter stroked his cock through his track-pants and nodded at her to do as she was told.

Jack scrubbed his face, looking almost annoyed with her for letting him feel—lust? Was there a glimpse, though so brief, of lust for her in his eyes? The thought gave her hope.

She rose onto her knees then leaned down toward the small puddle. She had never tasted herself before. She never got to really explore herself sexually when she was by herself because the thought she was undesirable doused everything for her.

But here and now, she had three gorgeous intelligent men hard for her, wanting her to lick up her own juices. They made her feel brave and hot and sexy.

She lowered her head. Carter leaned forward to get a better view. Caleb's voice, soft and husky, made her pause.

"Lick it up, all of it but don't swallow it. I want you to pour it on the tip of my cock and then lick it off again before you swallow."

They were intent on killing her.

She did as she was told, slurping up her liquid and holding it in her mouth. She heard their groans and felt the arousal shroud her. She then turned and faced Caleb again.

"Hands behind your back," he said as he positioned his cock for her. "Now pour your juice all over my cock, princess."

Saffron let her essence fall from her mouth and onto him. She held her hands tightly behind her back, digging her nails into her palm so she didn't come, didn't climax just from this act alone.

"Now suck it up and swallow it, baby. I want to see you swallow."

She licked and sucked and drew all her wetness from him then, raising her eyes, she lifted her chin and swallowed. That seemed to be too much for Caleb. He gripped her hair and slid into her mouth, wasting no time fucking her.

"Ah, fuck," he grunted. "Hold me deep, Saffron. I want to slip straight down your throat."

Her eyes watered. The swell of sensation inside her burst. She'd never felt prouder in her life than now, and when Carter had made her swallow his come. Caleb held her head still, deep in her throat. She was gagging but breathing through her nose. He stiffened and then, looking into her eyes, he ejaculated and she took her time swallowing everything he gave her.

He picked her up when she was done and kissed her soundly. He carried her to their bedroom where he laid her down on her tummy. He then massaged her back and the backs of her thighs and her feet. He covered her searing backside with the soothing balm Carter had used and played with her hair until she fell asleep, which didn't take very long at all.

WHEN SAFFRON AWOKE the next morning, she stretched and smiled and happiness washed over her. Until a black cloud hovered over her head. Today was Jack's turn to ensure she never deceived them again by giving her a god-awful hard spanking from which she would get hopelessly turned on. But would he? A niggling feeling settled in her tummy and refused to leave her.

She wasn't as confident in her ability with Jack since he held her at such a distance, not the way she was with Carter and Caleb. Last night when he'd got aroused, it had been fleeting—and she might have imagined it anyway, which was more likely. So, she was basically back at square one with him. He didn't even sleep in the same room with her and Carter and Caleb.

She slipped into a pair of the track-pants and a t-shirt again and went downstairs. She never expected to see the sight that greeted her.

"For fuck's sake, Caleb, throw those away and get new ones. You're hurting my eyes with all that glitter," Carter said, shielding his eyes. And there stood Caleb, completely bare except for one of the briefs she had upgraded, eating breakfast. She burst out laughing. Okay, so it had backfired. He didn't get mad at her at all. But still, to see him actually wearing it, that just tickled her funny bone.

"Good morning, princess. Like my new look?" he asked. God, he was gorgeous. Pure muscle, no fat on abs, chest, biceps or thighs. "So, at least now you know, huh?" He pointed to above his crotch where she had written *my cock is bigger than my IQ* and splattered it with glitter and sequins.

Definitely backfired.

He grabbed her and kissed her, bringing her onto his thick cock.

"Not what you expected to happen when you went turning my boxers into some sort of rainbow, pony, kitty land thing?"

She shook her head, smiling.

"Good. I live to remain a surprise." He pulled in a deep breath. "One more night and we get to break into that pussy," he added softly.

Seriously, she needed to remain dry for at least a couple of hours a day, or else how was she going to think? She woke up aroused, she went to bed aroused. She was constantly aroused.

"Where's Jack?" she asked when Caleb released her.

Carter took her into his arms next and answered her. "He left already."

"Oh," she said, trying not to be hurt. Both Carter and Caleb had given her instructions regarding her punishment spanking the last two mornings and now, when it was Jack's turn to do the same, he conveniently wasn't around. Could he make himself any clearer? He didn't want her. Well, not the way Carter and Caleb did.

"Jack's complicated. He'll come around, sweetheart." Carter kissed her again then released her.

"But it's me, isn't it?" The guys looked at each other. She didn't need to be a rocket scientist to see she was Jack's biggest and only problem. "If he doesn't like me, will he be a part of when you.. when we..." After everything they made her do and say and feel she still felt uncannily shy around them sometimes.

"He'll definitely be a part of when we get you pregnant, Saffron. We all needed to be in accordance or it wouldn't happen. Just give him some time." Carter touched her cheek.

"But it is me, personally, on some level, right?" She turned to Caleb. Carter had a way of trying to protect her. Caleb told her the truth.

"Yes," Caleb said.

"Fine," she said nodding. It really hurt to hear her suspicions confirmed by someone she trusted already with her life. Was that crazy? *Spank me, make me suck your cock and I'll trust you for life.* That's what happened with Carter and Caleb exactly. Maybe she was crazy.

"It'll be fine," Caleb said gently as he put on his jeans and shirt which graced the back of a chair. She continued nodding. Once they left, she sat at the kitchen table and tried to understand the lump in her throat.

She couldn't even bring herself to eat the delicious breakfast Carter had prepared for her. Jack's feelings toward her shattered her.

She dragged herself upstairs after a sip of juice and a slice of toast. It was Friday and the two Anns would not be coming again until next week, Monday. She really could have done with the company.

After removing her plug, she stepped into the shower. She let the hot water hit her hard, standing there for what felt like an hour, even long after she had lathered herself thrice. The sting in her backside reminded her of her hot night with Caleb and even Jack's dilemma failed to stop her pussy from dampening. She closed her eyes and imagined the three of them coming for her. Cocks hard and ready. Spreading her. Making her wetter. She remembered when Jack had inserted the thermometer into her backside and she gasped. Tonight, he would be inserting the biggest butt plug of all.

She imagined feeling their cum inside her. She touched her belly imagining their baby growing inside her. She imagined Carter's face as he ejaculated into her, telling her how happy he was that she came in her sister's place. Caleb's face as he came inside her, telling her the same thing as Carter. Glad it was her. And then there was Jack.

Her eyes flew open. Was that the reason Jack didn't like her, didn't want her?

Anger replaced her hurt. The same anger she had turned to when her boyfriend, Paul McAndrews had left her with her legs parted in the middle of the night.

She stepped out the shower. She was fuming by the time she dried herself. Well, Jack was going to hear a piece of her mind whether he liked it or not.

She pulled out her favorite skirt, the black and red plaid mini, a white shirt on which she rolled the sleeves up and a pair of her wedge boots. She grabbed her hair into a pony tail and searched her handbag for her car keys.

She had seen a map up in the study of where they were working. She took a picture with her phone. A million spikes of sensation ripped through her as she saw a chart with her cycle right next to the map on the wall. The date she had her last period and when she'd be fertile marked with x's. Most people got turned on watching porn. She got turned on by seeing the cycle of her period up on the wall of their study marked with the days they planned to have her. She'd be ovulating in three days' time. She let that thought sink in. It would be possible for her to become pregnant with their baby in three days' time. Three days' time.

By the time she got into her car, she was blushing profusely. But first she had to let Jack know exactly what was on her mind.

The paths were clearly marked and she paid extra attention not to get lost. She had to have this thing out with Jack ASAP. It was eating her alive.

Finally, she arrived at the site, thankful her car didn't stop altogether in the middle of nowhere and leave her stranded for the bears to eat. Once she got out of the car, she attracted all kinds of attention. Whistles and cat-calls and all kinds of stupid salutations.

One older nice-looking man came up to her.

"Hi there, Miss. I'm Tom. Are you lost, Miss?" He turned and told the rest of the crew to shut up as he could barely hear himself talk with all their wolf-whistles.

"No. My name is Saffron and I'm looking for Jack Hallson?"

"Jack. He's down that way, Miss. Let me get him for you, it's pretty dangerous out here, Miss."

"I'll be fine, Tom, thank you." And with that she marched off in the direction Tom had pointed. She ignored him rushing up after her and telling her how dangerous it was for her to be there.

"Jack," she called. "Jack."

"What the fuck," Jack said as he came toward her. "What the hell are you doing here, woman? Do you know how dangerous this is?"

Just then Carter arrived followed closely by Caleb, the rage in their eyes matched Jack's.

"You don't even have a helmet on." Jack shouted at her, then proceeded to remove his helmet and shoved it onto her head.

"What the hell are you doing here, Saffron?" Carter roared.

"Do you want to get yourself killed?" Caleb growled at her.

Taking her by an arm each, both Jack and Caleb pulled her along toward a truck.

"What are you doing?" She tried to stall them but they were mountains on either side of her. "I came here to tell you, Jack, to go to hell. You can't make me feel—"

"Tom," Carter called. "Take her home. And don't let her talk you out of anything." She had never really seen Carter so mad at her.

Jack shoved her into the truck. "You'll be lucky if I don't take a cane to you instead of my belt. You'll wait in my rooms, naked and kneeling on the floor as you waited for Carter and Caleb and now for me," he said darkly.

Saffron blushed painfully. Tom heard every word of Jack's threat. And so did everyone else close by. She opened her mouth to gain her pride back.

"Not another word from you. Give me your keys." And just like that, her panties dampened, her heart ached and her mind just wanted to obey him. If only he wanted her submission. But she felt miserable. She had made a scene, embarrassed them in front of their employees. How were they going to deal with her rashness?

After giving him her car keys, she got into a company truck with Tom and remained silent the whole way back to the house. But Tom tried to have a conversation with her.

"You're Alan Sinclair's daughter, aren't you?" he asked.

"Yes, I am. Do you know him?"

"I do. We have a chat now and again when I see him at—" He paused.

"Montgomery's," Saffron finished for him.

"Yes," Tom said, flushed.

"Well I hope you try to stay away from that place. Montgomery is evil. He is the whole reason I'm here." Her misery had reached new heights now. Tom nodded, but said nothing.

"I'm sorry, Miss. I hope it doesn't hurt too much," he said sincerely just before she got out of the truck.

Crimson now, she mumbled a thank you and hurried away. Once inside she threw herself onto her bed and spent the next few hours telling herself why she wasn't allowed to cry. Because she was all cried out after Paul had left her so devastatingly. He had ruined her confidence and Jack was doing the same. How could Carter and Caleb be so interested in her, want her so badly, touch her and kiss her so tenderly and yet so demandingly and how can Jack not want to do any of those things with her? Well, she figured it out. And it hurt her even more.

Eventually she forced herself to get up, to get something to eat. She took a bath next to while away the time then went into Jack's room much earlier than she normally did. She waited, smelling like roses, kneeling in his doctor's room, waiting for them.

They surprised her by getting there earlier and when Jack entered first, relief seeped into her. Was she that needy that she would take a belting from him rather than nothing at all? She also understood the bond Carter and Caleb shared with Jack. It was real and strong and impenetrable. They came in threes. Not as individuals even though they were so different in personality. They were one and she needed them as one.

They had showered as usual, fresh male soap and cologne filled her nostrils. Even through her turmoil, her wetness continued to grow.

She looked at Carter and Caleb. Their disappointment shone through in their eyes. They weren't mad at her anymore. But their disappointment was even worse. She couldn't bear it.

"Explain," Carter said. Her indignation returned. Her pride flared. Oh, she would explain all right. She started to rise. "Back on your knees," Carter said.

Really? How was she supposed to show her anger, demonstrate that she didn't care what Jack thought of her when she remained on her knees. She couldn't be flippant this way. Oh, right. That's exactly why they wanted her on her knees, they didn't want any theatrics.

"Now tell us why you recklessly put your life at risk by entering a very active felling operation. What made you decide to do something like that? What was it you came all the way to tell Jack? We all want to know." Then as if he couldn't contain his calm anymore, "Explain why you decided to think it was a good idea to come to the site without even a goddamn helmet on, putting your life in danger and scaring the fucking shit out of all three of us."

She remained silent. How could they make her feel horrible for her actions even if her reasoning was right? They cared about her. Except Jack.

She didn't even know how to start. Being on her knees changed the angle of her attack on Jack. She lowered her head. "I know why he doesn't like me and I just wanted to tell him he could... he could go to hell, because I wasn't going to be bothered with him anymore."

"And why do you think Jack doesn't like you?" Caleb asked.

"Because I wasn't what he expected. Because I look like this and he, he wanted my sister instead who is beautiful and sweet and smart. And I'm not," she murmured.

Jack's laughter brought her head straight up again. She didn't say anything funny at all. Carter rubbed his neck and Caleb looked down. But Jack? Jack's laughter crept under her skin and titillated her nerves. He had the most sexy, huskiest laugh she had ever heard from any man. Maybe because she had heard Carter and Caleb's laughter before and never Jack's. In fact, she had wondered if he ever laughed, or even smiled at all. Now it was the most beautiful sound in the world. Until she remembered why he was laughing.

"You think I don't like you because I had my heart set on your sister?" Jack asked when he brought his laughter down to a grin.

"Yes, exactly. But you're stuck with me and I can't help that and Marigold has her own life and, and—"

"I don't want your sister. I never did."

She frowned up at him, completely naked. "But you still don't like me." God, she sounded like an insecure child. *Like me, Jack.*

*Please like me, Jack.* She believed him when he said he wasn't disappointed she'd come in her sister's place. He didn't want Marigold. But he also didn't want her—except to carry his baby.

"If ever you find out why I treated you the way I did, you'll be happy I don't like you, Saffron." His harsh words were tinged with sadness and she wanted to leap into his arms and hug him. He dismissed her then turned toward Carter. "I'm ready," he said. The look Carter gave him held everything. From fierce protectiveness. To hope. What wasn't Jack telling her? His cryptic words hurt her heart. She couldn't think of anything that would make him say those peculiar words to her.

"Saffron," Carter said formally. "It's Jack's turn now to complete your punishment regarding deception, particularly that you will never deceive us ever again.

She looked down. "Yes, Sir."

"Stand up, Saffron," Jack said. Was he not going to spank her then? Didn't he want her to crawl after him? Her heart sank a little. Until he started to unbuckle the belt on his jeans. Unlike Carter and Caleb, he always wore jeans even after he came home and showered. Her mouth dried. Her pussy wept and ached and she felt as if she might just collapse back onto her knees and just beg—beg for everything. Beg to be placed into their care, to be told what to do, how to do it. How could she have changed so much so quickly?

"Bend over my desk," he ordered. She missed a breath, but obediently bent over.

"Move further away from the desk. I want you to have to stand on your toes." She glowed at Jack giving her instructions. What to do, how to place her body. She needed this even though his issue with her remained unresolved.

"Keep your legs closed, Saffron, tightly closed, even when I push the plug into you," he said softly. He lifted her ass cheek and lubed her up. Nervousness swept over her. This one would be the biggest. He massaged the lube into her ass. She quivered with need until he started to stuff her with the plug. She swallowed her pain as he stretched her. But she purred when he ran a hand down her back over her ass. He was touching her. Touching her not to give her a clinical exam like he did before but to insert a butt plug into her and spank her. Her mind imploded with the hotness of that thought.

"Brace yourself, girl," he issued before his belt found her ass and whipped her thoroughly. "You'll take six strikes and for every one, one you'll repeat the words, 'I will never deceive my men'. Do you understand?"

"Yes, Sir."

"Do you remember your safeword?"

"Yes, Sir."

"Good." He punctuated his approval with another streak of sheer pain.

Saffron bit back the tears stinging in her eyes. "I will never deceive my men."

Number three followed that one and she slumped a little. And yet the only thought going through her head was how much she wanted them to touch her pussy. Her sexual craze had reached an unbearable, unthinkable high. This kind of pain had morphed inside her and opened up avenues she didn't know she possessed.

"You're taking this well, Saffron. Just three more."

"Yes, Sir." She basked under his praise, tilting her head this way and that way as she sought Carter and Caleb. They knew she looked for them and came into her view. She sighed heavily with thanks. Like this, she could get through anything.

Four and five happened in quick succession. She was shaking, a mixture of learning her lesson and wanting to give herself over to them to do with as they pleased.

She would never deceive them again. Not for all the money in the world. Not for anything. Not even for Marigold or her father. She had done that before, sacrificed for her family to have a great life. But now nothing would make her turn against these lumberjacks.

The only thing that got her through number six was Jack's hand on her lower back.

Once she repeated the words, he brought her up against him, holding her arms as she leaned her head against his shoulder, the solid strength of his body against her back. His breath lingered on her neck. As if he were torn between kissing her and not. He released her all too quickly.

She spun around to watch him heading for the door. Nothing could have prepared her for the bitter pain slashing her heart. He didn't want her to thank him for her belting? Her eyes filled with tears, but she swiped them away quickly. She wasn't going to let him get off this easily.

"Jack," she called after him. He slowed for a second and then continued walking. "Jack," she shouted, all her anger and frustration poured into his name.

He turned around and she backed into the desk. Enigmatic Jack no longer existed. In his place was a man who was contorted with anger and frustration himself.

"What? You want to thank me for your belting, Saffron? Are you sure you can handle this?"

He pulled off his t-shirt and shoved his jeans and boxer-briefs down.

Saffron gasped.

# CHAPTER 9

*S*affron's heart tore to pieces in her chest. Jack, gorgeous and sexy Jack. His upper body was a map of scars, going down to his left thigh just at his penis where his deepest biggest scar could be found.

The scars were old, some embedded and embossed into his skin. She could tell they all happened in his early childhood. She wanted to kill the person who had done that to him with her bare hands. Rage for him swelled inside her.

Oh, Jack.

Is that the reason he thought she would be grateful he didn't like her? Because of his scars? How little did he think of her? Did she come off as that superficial? He didn't know her at all. And the moment Carter and Caleb came to stand at his sides, protecting him, shielding him from the world, her heart just burst with emotion. Jack didn't need any protection. He was big and strong and could be very bad and he could handle himself, she knew that. But the bond the three friends had forged during childhood stood clear and tall and impenetrable. But they needn't protect him against her. He didn't need to protect himself against her. Not ever.

"Jack," she whispered. He bent to pick up his t-shirt and at the same time, his face hardened. She went toward him and stood in front of him. A single tear slipped down her face. His jaw clenched so hard she felt the tension in his body.

She reached out her hand and ran her fingers over the deep, twisted gashes on his chest. He didn't even breathe at her touch. Never had he looked more beautiful to her. His body was one she wanted to explore with her hands, her mouth, her everything.

She started to lower herself onto her knees but he caught her arm and brought her flush against his body. Her nipples hardened against his chest. Her pussy pulsed.

"I don't need your pity," he growled at her.

She looked up at him. "This isn't pity, Jack. This is my need," she whispered. She placed her lips on his and kissed him softly. His unresponsiveness didn't deter her. She licked his lip and pressed her hot naked body to him. His cock twitched against her and he growled deep in his throat before he forced his tongue into her mouth and kissed her brains out. He pulled her against him, and deepened the kiss tenfold harder. By the time he released her she was breathless.

She let her knees bend forcing him to let her go down as she kneeled in front of him.

"Thank you, Sir, for my punishment." She put her hands behind her back and licked the head of his cock. Jack threw his head back when she engulfed him, then released him. She sucked along his shaft, she kissed the scar on his thigh, the one that was so close to his beautiful cock, the painful brand deep and long. He gripped her hair and pulled her head back as if she had done something wrong. For moments, he stared down at her. She opened her mouth for him and after grunting in pure frustration, he brought her head back to his stunning cock.

She sighed as his pre-cum coated her tongue and ignited her taste buds. She sucked him with all she had, taking him deeper into her throat than ever before. And not once did she stop looking at him.

Something came over her. She couldn't explain except to say it resembled such a rush of emotion she wanted to cry in joy. Jack was giving her this. He completed her now. The feeling so strong surged through her and it became a medley of lust and need and urgency and intensity.

Carter put his hand on her shoulder and squeezed. In that touch, she felt his thanks. Caleb stroked his knuckles down her cheek as she deep-throated Jack to show her thanks. Didn't they know she needed this? Wayward her, who kept her emotions hidden, her sexuality a lie, needed them, it wasn't the other way around.

Jack stilled and tried to pull out of her mouth. Didn't he know that was not how it was done? She pulled harder on him. Her gaze pleading with him to stay inside her.

"Fuck," he roared and allowed himself to come down her throat. She didn't have any technique, any skill, certainly zero experience, except for Carter and Caleb, but she had desire. Desire to please them and she did everything she could to achieve that.

She swallowed his copious amount of cum. He held her with both hands now cupping the sides of her head. Slowly he withdrew from her mouth, but the instant his still hard cock left her lips, she sucked him back inside. Jack's groan delighted her. His cock twitched deliciously as she finally let him have it back.

The tension in the room grew thicker. She sat back, her ankles reminding her of her very sore, belted behind. Of the huge plug in her ass.

"Will you let me fuck you, the way I am, Saffron? Naked, with all my revolting scars for you to see?"

She had a speech ready for him, how she thought he was crazy beautiful and now that she knew he wasn't rejecting her because he didn't like her but because he didn't know how she would react to the scars on his body, she thought him even more beautiful because he made her feel that way now.

She wanted to say so much and be angry at him at the same time for thinking she was so shallow that she would run from him in revulsion. Had someone done that to him before? She would kill the woman who made him feel less.

"Yes, Sir. Please, Sir," she said instead.

"Don't you find me off-putting? Do you want me to put my clothes back on while the three of us fuck you?"

He seemed to want her to say no to him. "Please, no, Sir. I want to be able to touch you. Every part of you. Of all of you."

He paused in thought before he continued. "Is your pussy wet?" Jack asked. Why did he have to be so thoroughly sure about her wanting it right now with him as he was.

"Yes, Sir."

"Why?"

Why? He wanted to know why she was wet? Had he seen what she'd been put through the last three days? Touched and kissed and even the punishments turned her on. But his question made another truth dawn on her: in the moment Jack revealed why he didn't want to touch her because he thought she would be revolted if he did; in the moment she saw his body and understood his reason; in the moment she looked at the three of them, Carter, Jack and Caleb, standing next to each other, regarding her while she kneeled naked in front of them; in that moment she understood everything about herself.

"I'm not very experienced, Sir. I only pretend to be sexy and sexual. The clothes, the hair, the piercings and tattoos, they keep people away from me and they think I have a reputation. The truth is I am undesirable. I don't know how to really be sexy. I don't know what to do with myself. But you and Carter and Caleb tell me what to do and it makes me feel as if only I exist and I'm the sexiest woman alive. The most desirable. I can't be those things without the three of you," she finished softly. She had her own scars to deal with. But she'd put her desires in their hands and needed their direction.

Silence ensued in the room as they observed her. She had never been more honest in her whole life. She needed them. Before they entered her life, she faked everything she couldn't avoid. Would they think less of her now? Maybe they thought she was undesirable, just like Paul did, and really were only getting their money's worth at all costs. Maybe she started to romanticize this and they were keeping it real

The thought had her straightening her spine and raising her chin. She had opened up to them—stupidly. They didn't find her sexy. She was just about to get up and run away when Jack's words stopped her.

"Show us."

She looked blankly at him.

"Show us how wet you are for us, Saffron."

She exhaled, she really didn't know what to expect with them anymore. They surprised her continuously.

She rose onto her knees, parted her legs and scooped out her wetness, shuddering as she penetrated the swollen folds of her pussy. She'd been gushing with desire for too long now.

Jack came to crouch down in front of her. He took her hand, sticky and silky wet to his nose. He inhaled deeply, holding her hand for long moments. He licked his lips and her heart thundered. She thought he would suck on her fingers. She closed her eyes, imagining his tongue twirling around her digits. Her pussy felt every imaginary tug, nip, and lick.

"Please," she whimpered, pleading with them to not let this end. For Jack to believe her.

He continued to regard her. The dejection inside her rose. She was losing him. He glanced at his shoulder draped with a deep long scar as if to remind himself. He released her hand, rose, picked up his t-shirt from the floor and turned toward the door again. What more did she have to say to him? He completely broke her heart.

"Jack," Carter called in a voice she had never heard him use before. Jack paused for a second before he continued. "Jack," Carter said again, "we take her now." Jack stopped this time completely, but he didn't turn around. "Now," Carter said with dangerous authority. Jack turned and looked at her. Tears slid down her face.

"Fuck," Jack roared as he threw his t-shirt to the floor and charged toward her. He picked her up from the floor in one fluid motion. He forced her legs around his waist, holding her with one arm around her waist.

"Fuck," he said again. "Fuck, fuck, fuck." He fumbled with his jeans and then suddenly Caleb came in behind her, holding her up for Jack while he released his cock.

He drove into her. She gasped and slammed back against Caleb, her solid anchor keeping her safe. Jack's penetration took the breath from her. The long deep thrust awakened and stretched her. She froze for a second, looking for Carter who stood close by. The sight of him made her brave.

She hadn't gotten this far before. No man had ever buried himself so deep inside her. Had ever been this thick, this hot inside her. She softened for him, wetter than ever, relaxed her muscles and moved until he was completely embedded inside her.

"Fuck," Jack whispered almost angrily. "Fuck," he said this time defeated as he withdrew and then penetrated her again. She moaned, keeping her gaze fixed on him. She clutched at his cock and he grew larger inside her. They kept the butt plug Jack had put into her still inside her. It made her feel all the more full.

Jack grunted and crushed his lips against hers, sending her back into Caleb's chest, his cock hard and strong against her ass, reminding her of where Jack had belted her, adding so many more layers to what she felt right that minute.

Jack sucked her lips, he kissed her jaw, nipped at the side of her throat. He brushed his thumb across a nipple and she shuddered around his cock. He pulled out and looked down to between their bodies to see his cock slip into her again, hard. She gasped and he held her head and kissed her even harder.

His momentum increased. He sent her hurtling against Caleb who stood like a pillar of stone behind her.

"She's the one, Jack," Caleb said. "What she did today, coming after you like that, out there, even if she didn't know how dangerous it was. The girl was jealous, Jack, she thought you wanted her sister."

Jack thrust harder into her. She was close to coming. *Please, Jack. Please, now.*

"We couldn't have asked for a better girl," Carter said gruffly. "What more do you need from her, Jack?" Carter's voice softened.

Jack's gaze hadn't left hers as he slid and slipped inside her. She wished with her all her heart he could see how much she needed him too, his whole naked warmth to complete her. Everything about him. And Carter and Caleb.

"Everything," Jack said at last staring into her eyes. "I need everything from her." She raised her head to lock her gaze with his. His hand curled around her throat. "Give me everything, Saffron, give us every part of you." The air around her disintegrated and all that remained was one woman and the three men who needed her everything. "Caleb," Jack said, his tone filled with intense, dark need.

"I got you, bro." Caleb slipped his hand between their bodies. His fingers slid to her clit where he tapped her then started to vigorously rub at her. Her insides turned to jelly. Jack's cock pushed deeper and deeper inside her.

"I want to feel you coming around my cock. Come for me, Saffron so I'll know this," he said, and picked up her hand, laying it over his heart, "doesn't revolt you."

She knew he wanted her to feel his scars. She felt beyond that to his heart instead.

"Jack." His name fell from her lips brokenly and thirstily. He thrust into her, touching a part of her that made her clit soar under Caleb's hand and sent her over the edge. She burst from within, her climax long and hard and taking everything from her. And she poured all that into Jack.

"Saffron," he whispered. His body stiffened. He held her so close against him. She kissed him and wrapped her arms around his neck and let him empty himself inside her. The warmth of his cum filled her as he shuddered and shuddered and shuddered again for her. Carter took Caleb's place behind her. Jack kissed her one last time before he slipped out of her and before she could even feel a moment of emptiness, or coldness, Caleb was there, his cock hard, big and ready. He slipped into her easily.

"Caleb," she could only say his name.

"I'm right here, princess," he murmured, his cock grinding into her.

"Caleb's going to take care of you," Carter said, cupping her breast with his one hand, his thumb continuously brushing her nipple.

"I need to… I need to again. Please." She couldn't think straight. She only needed to come again. With Caleb.

"I know, princess. Can you feel my cock, feel how big it is inside you? I'm going to blow soon and you're going to come all around me. I'm going to feel your pussy clench."

Carter pinched then pulled at her nipple. Caleb moved a little back, tilted her a little, his hands on her hips as Carter held her up for him with one arm around her waist. She glanced down to see his cock pounding in and out of her.

"Jack," she said almost deliriously as Caleb continued to hammer his cock into her. Jack was at her side instantly. She clutched his cock, still semi-hard as he brought his hand to her clit, his lips to the side of her neck where he drew her flesh into his mouth and sucked. Being this close to them, being in the center of them made her feel like their universe. As if she were that important to them. If only.

Jack increased his rhythm on her clit. Caleb deepened his cock inside her. Her climax started to take a hold of her. She cried out, whimpering, sobbing as she exploded. Caleb roared, threw his head back and came inside her. Hard. Jack removed his hand. Caleb then took her from Carter. Held her tightly as he finished coming, her legs wrapped around his waist. Perspiration gleamed from their bodies as he carried her through a door in Jack's doctor's room.

He laid her down on a bed as big as the one upstairs, kissing her as he slowly withdrew.

"Carter," Caleb said and again, she was immediately taken by Carter. He lifted her legs. Jack and Caleb's cum had started to seep from her. She was so wet and so full of their cum and her own. But Carter just used the head of his cock to scoop up the cum dripping from her and put it back inside her. He then kept it inside her by plugging her with his cock. She didn't understand why that mattered to her so much. Why his act both blew her already blown mind and turned her on and made her feel whole and empowered at the same time. But it was just like Carter. He'd keep everything together no matter what. That's why their bond with each other was so strong and she wanted to be a part of that strength. She wanted to earn her keep and offer her body whichever way they wanted her.

She slid up the bed as Carter penetrated her. He did so slowly, filling her inch by inch until he was completely embedded inside her. He knelt and kept her legs up against each of his shoulders.

"So fucking tight. So fucking perfect," he whispered. Her fever grew. She became restless until Jack and Caleb stood at her head and Carter pushed her towards the edge of the bed where his friends could feed her their cocks. She sucked hungrily. Held them to her face. Kissed them and licked them. That they were hard for her again thrilled her.

Carter's thrust became more forceful. Her breasts bounced. Jack licked his fingers and skimmed her nipple. Carter found her clit, the tips of his fingers working to make her come again. And then it started again. Everything was perfect. Carter's cock inside her. Jack and Caleb's cocks in her mouth. Her third climax began and it still felt like her first, as if she hadn't come twice already around two thick rock-hard cocks.

She shuddered and spasmed for Carter until he roared.

"I'm going to come." He lowered himself, towering over her before he slipped a hand under her butt, brought her closer and ejaculated inside her, his face nestled against her neck. Saffron held him, waiting until he emptied himself inside her. He rolled off her then immediately cupped her pussy. She tightened her thighs with his hand still between them. Caleb still standing at her head, leaned down and kissed her upside down. A deep wet kiss that left her even more breathless.

"You okay? Did we hurt you?" Carter asked.

She shook her head, then kissed him.

"Open your legs, sweetheart, I want to remove the plug. You did well taking us with it still inside you." He slowly removed the plug Jack had put inside her earlier before her belting. Her muscles relaxed instantly but she felt empty without it.

Jack slipped in next to her and she turned to kiss him, too. Carter then drew her against his chest, and within a heartbeat her eyes drifted closed. She slept soundly, even when they changed in whose arms she slept. It was as if they worked in shifts the whole night long to hold her.

She seemed to sleep forever, finally waking when morning was already almost over. She was alone but a note lay on the pillow. Instantly their absence made her miss them so severely her heart threatened to pop. She was instructed to have breakfast and relax in the tub, maybe even sleep more if she wanted. She glanced around the room and found a table had been set with a scrumptious brunch.

Wrapping herself in the sheet, she skipped to the table and gobbled up whatever she wanted. Salmon and sushi and little chicken wraps. She ate a handful of blackberries and drank her power smoothie—the one Carter always made for her, meant to fortify her for when she became pregnant. Pregnant with their baby.

She never ever once in her life thought about children. Well, she had, but she decided she would make the worst mother ever. But now along with the butterfly feeling in her stomach about having their baby, something else nagged at her. Maybe that they paid for her? Did she forget that part? She doubted they did. They weren't the type of men to get sidelined from their ultimate goal. More to the point, she didn't have enough allure to keep them interested. Sadly.

But last night was amazing. They were demanding and yet careful with her, hard yet gentle. That's just the way they were, it wasn't because she brought those qualities out of them. She shook her head to clear it of all nonsensical romantic notions she seemed to be acquiring for them. She still remained Saffron Sinclair. The girl whose boyfriend had been so turned-off by her he fled while in the middle of penetration. Carter, Caleb, and Jack took her last night because they paid for her. She must never forget that. She needed to go back to being sassy-ass Saffron. Not this girl with her head bouncing about in the clouds. She wasn't that person. This was a business deal.

Feeling despondent and angry at herself for losing her head, she took an extra-long shower to make sure she never forgot her place with them. That they'd brought her toiletries down to this room and that made her smile, until she forced herself to wipe it right off her face.

She smothered her skin in lotion and looked around for her gown, or anything, to wear. Finding nothing, she wrapped the sheet around herself again, her intent to go upstairs and put on proper clothes.

Her hand stilled on the door knob. Their voices, though soft, could be heard from the other side. They were talking about her.

## CHAPTER 10

*S*affron strained to listen. There was a pause. She heard Jack sigh deeply before he said. "I know. I underestimated her. And she surprised me," he continued softly. He sighed again. "She surprised the fuck out of me. She's different. I expected her to run in the opposite direction. Instead, ah hell, she took my cock into her mouth."

"And how fucking tight is she?" Caleb asked. "I thought I was going to die when I got inside her pussy."

"And when she came." Jack laughed softly. "Those tiny little spasms feeding along our cocks, fuck, she is everything, isn't she? Stubborn, saucy, reckless too. So in need of punishments."

Carter laughed. "She's perfect. A handful. She needs the three of us to keep her in line, that's for sure. Any chance of her getting pregnant after last night, Jack?"

"She's not ovulating for the next two days, but it's possible she could be. It's not an exact science."

Saffron touched her belly. Was she pregnant right now?

"I say we play with her first. And get to the bottom of why she thinks she's not desirable, whatever the fuck that means," Carter said. "How do you feel about that, Jack? Just say the word and we keep it clean."

Jack laughed that beautiful laugh of his. "We going to clean her out first?" he asked.

*Clean her out?* What exactly did that mean?

"Fuck yeah," Caleb added, with pure delight in his voice. "We're going to take as long as we like with her. We have all the time in the world."

"Let's get started then," Carter ended their discussion. "Saffron," he called. "We know you're standing behind the door, sweetheart, and eavesdropping on us. Come out now."

Okay, was the door transparent or something? She had half a mind to jump into the bed and pretend she was sleeping. They wouldn't believe her though. She opened the door and stepped out.

"Drop the sheet," Caleb instructed. "There's a reason we didn't bring you any clothes. We want you naked at all times."

She swallowed. Well, good morning to you, too.

The sheet slithered to the floor. She stood perfectly still, shy even now after they had all had a chance with her. Everyday seemed to be like that with them.

"Come here," Carter said. She started toward him. It was hard not to notice their cocks had grown as their gazes slid down her body.

"Kneel," Jack said.

Instantly she dropped to her knees. Okay, obeying them was getting a little too easy for her.

Carter rose from the sofa he'd been lounging on. He crouched down in front of her.

"We're going to play with you today, sweetheart. You're going to be screaming our names by the time we're done with you. We're going to fuck you and we plan to fuck you hard and deep and fast and long and rough and gentle and tender and as many times as we want in any fucking hole we want. And you're going to tell us why you think you're undesirable. You're going to tell us everything. Do you understand?"

"Yes, Sir," she whispered, her body and lips trembling. And so much wetness already now flooding her. But how could she tell them about her ex-boyfriend. What if they laughed at her?

"Again, do you understand what we're saying to you?"

"Yes, Sir," she said so softly she barely heard her own voice.

"You remember your safeword?"

She nodded. She couldn't utter another word, not with her body on fire the way it was.

Caleb came to her and scooped her up. A bunch of nerves settled in her tummy. Caleb must have detected her nervousness as he carried her to that torture chair again where Jack had examined her so intimately and yet so professionally on her second day with them.

"It's all right, princess. You just do whatever we tell you to do. All right? We got this. We got you, okay?" She nodded and tightened her arms around his neck all the same. What if she disappointed them? This was the real test, wasn't it? Last night had been passionate and they didn't get to see her flaws properly. But before she could analyze it any further, Caleb placed her down on her feet beside the bench.

"Up and on all fours like the time we took your temperature, princess."

She blushed even more thinking about that episode. Had she been perpetually wet since then? No, she had been since the moment she sat in their study.

"Jack's going to give you an enema," Carter said, standing on the other side of her, and she nearly fell off the chair. "Relax, sweetheart, he's a doctor. He knows what he's doing."

She gripped the edges of the chair with all her strength as Carter slid the cuffs around her wrists, keeping her bound to it. God, what was going to happen to her? The little bit of fear of the unknown, increased by her helplessness, added a new layer to her arousal. How could she be into these kinds of things? Who was she?

Situated as she was on all fours, it was easy for Caleb to get behind her. He then parted her ass-cheeks. "Still soaking wet," he observed when he looked at her pussy. "Does this turn you on, princess? Us subjecting you to such an experience while we watch Jack fill your ass and let you keep it in there until we say you're ready? Huh? Tell me, princess," Caleb insisted.

"Yes, Sir." The truth escaped her before she could deny it.

"Look at that ass. Perfect."

Carter traced the now faint stripes of Jack's belt marks on her backside and at once he triggered the delicious memory of the whipping sting she had felt not so long ago. She shuddered and shook.

"She was made for this. Made for us, to play with, to fuck," Carter added.

Oh god. Where was Jack? She twisted her head around to see what he was doing. And together with Carter and Caleb who had removed their t-shirts to show their stunning bodies, Jack was t-shirt-less too. His jeans hung low and the deep V of his abs was clearly visible. His power rippled as he moved. She still wanted to place kisses on every scar, big or small, on him.

That was it. She was going to die. She just couldn't handle them all even semi-naked. All that male beauty. All that power. All hers.

But for now, her heart stilled. Jack came toward her with a bag thingy attached to a nozzle thingy. She couldn't watch this, so she turned straight again and shut her eyes. Taking away her sight caused her to focus on the wetness trickling down her thigh. Why? How? This type of thing turned her on? No. They turned her on. And they were turned on, too. She had seen their cocks straining to break free of their pants and now their erections were enormous.

Did preparing the enema for her turn them on? Was it their domination over her? She loved being this helpless. Leaving everything up to them to decide on. She wasn't lying when she said she didn't know how to be sexual and ordinarily she never took orders from anyone. But these three men could order her to crawl to the end of the earth on her knees and she would do it.

"I want you to just relax, all right. It's your first time, I take it, so it's going to feel a little odd, but you'll get used to it after a while." Jack then lubed her ass while Carter and Caleb parted her cheeks. And she just dripped all the more. Holy cow. All their attention focused on her backside. How could she live through this?

"Ready?" Jack asked softly as he stroked her asshole. She nodded. "I'm going to need you to tell me, kitten." Kitten, was that his name for her? Carter called her sweetheart. Caleb princess. And Jack, kitten. She loved it.

"Yes, Sir. I'm ready," she said and immediately tensed.

Carter slapped her ass. "We told you to relax, not tense up, sweetheart."

She exhaled and allowed her muscles to give in. For her muscles trusted them as she herself already did. Jack pressed the nozzle against her hole.

"I'm not going to push it in very deep, kitten. Besides you've taken your biggest butt plug, you're just about ready for our cocks, so this will be nothing. You'll be fine, just breathe, all right?"

Again, she nodded before she used words and answered him. He slid it in a little further. She tried desperately not to tense again. It wasn't very thick so not entirely uncomfortable and like he said she was already accustomed to butt plugs. Soon she would be taking their cocks inside her there and from experience she knew how exceptionally big they were. That thought, however, poured more arousal into her.

Then he started to squirt the warm water inside her. The sensation was the oddest she had ever felt. Jack did so slowly, filling her bit by bit as Carter and Caleb caressed her ass and told her what a good little girl she was. How they were going to reward her with their cocks. How they were going to suck her clit until she couldn't come anymore.

They'd turned her into a feverish wreck. She was getting too full. She was too wet. Her pussy ached way too much. She needed relief. So badly. She planned to beg for it.

"All done, kitten," Jack said. "Now you just have to keep it inside you until I say you're ready. Do you understand?"

*Keep it inside me?*

How was she going to do that when all she wanted was to come hard—again and again and again.

"Keep it in you," Carter said and slapped her ass again. She quivered. Insanity waited around the next corner. And then that's how they left her, stranded there, ass in the air, trying her damnedest to keep the water inside her until she was told what to do next. They offered her water to drink and she refused. She couldn't do anything that would make her forget to hold it inside.

They took a seat on the biggest sofa in the room. She almost cried out in defeat when all three of them lifted their cocks out and started stroking them, their gazes on her. How could they do this to her? How could they be so mean when her wrists were bound and her pussy ached and her nipples needed their mouths, but she daren't even squeak in case she forgot to hold the water in.

The sight before her destroyed her mind. They were so amazingly, incredibly good-looking and now they were giving her a show. They played with their cocks, their eyes hazy. She could see the pre-cum glistening from their cockheads. She licked her lips. This torture was the worst they could ever subject her to.

And yet throughout this crazy-hot domination over her, she reveled in the three of them. All three of them, now that Jack had allowed her in. She wouldn't feel this way, this turned on, if he'd remained isolated from her.

She still wanted to tell him how beautiful she thought he was. That his scars were a part of him and all his parts fascinated her and thrilled her the same way Carter and Caleb's did. She wanted him to trust her. And she could only use her body to show him that. To let him do whatever he wanted to her.

But right now, she wanted to tell them she couldn't hold it any longer. Please could they fuck her now. Please, please, please.

Minutes ticked by. Or was it hours. Had she gone mad already? She needed to touch them right now.

Jack stood up, his cock still jutting from his jeans, wet with all the pre-cum he had worked onto his cock.

"All right?" he asked, cupping her face. She nodded. "Thirsty?"

"Yes, Sir," she said and leaned down toward his cock. His deep uneven inhalation encouraged her. She knew what he meant, but this was what she meant. She ran her tongue along his shaft, and tasted his pre-cum. She swallowed eagerly and went back for more.

Carter and Caleb came to her too. Caleb fondled her breasts and she sighed over Jack's cock.

Carter laid his hand against her pussy. "She's burning up," he said.

"Yeah, I know. Saffron, kitten, listen to me." Jack crouched to her level. "It's okay, kitten, we're going to take care of you. But first you need to go the bathroom, okay."

Saffron listened hard to Jack's instructions. Finally, she was going to get rid of the water inside her.

"We'll be waiting for you. Waiting to make you come, to fuck you—in your mouth, your pussy, your ass. Don't be too long," Jack said. She nodded and they unclasped her and helped her off the chair and into the bathroom.

She attended to herself, taking a shower to freshen up. The difference in her body could not be ignored. Maybe it was all mental, inside her head only, but she felt like a real woman, one who was desired. But when it came to it, would she disappoint them?

After she applied lotion, for the second time that morning, she stupidly looked for something to wear. There was nothing. They wanted her naked.

She took a deep breath and opened the bathroom door. She stepped into the room outside of the bedroom, naked, her body freshly cleaned and prettily scented. They had removed their clothes too and stilled when they saw her.

She shied away immediately. They would see what she was really about now. Undesirable? She lowered her head. How could she go from feeling like the hottest woman alive to the least in one second?

"Don't," Carter ordered her and she raised her face to look at them. "You're magnificent."

"You're the most stunning little thing we've ever seen," Caleb said.

"The most precious," Jack murmured.

She understood all their words, but Jack's had a double meaning. She accepted him for how he was, scars and all. He completed the circle.

"Come here," Carter ordered her. And so it began. She walked into his arms and was kissed thoroughly. Caleb and Jack stood at her side and kissed her neck. They played with her breasts and pinched her nipples until she was gasping for air. She reached out and touched their cocks. Her anchors. Her solace.

Caleb slapped her ass and she groaned, sucking even harder on Carter's tongue. He released her, then spun her around, her back to his chest, his cock rubbing against her ass. Jack kissed her then as Caleb engulfed her nipples. Carter held her by her arms, imprisoning her, keeping her still for his friends. His cock seemed gigantic behind her as he coated her butt with his pre-cum.

Caleb's fingers slipped into her pussy. She shuddered and Jack bit her lip until she cried out, an orgasm beginning to charge through her at full speed. So close, until Caleb slapped her clit and made her want to scream her frustration in foul language. More than that she wanted to claw at him. Force him to make her cum again. He laughed. She growled like an injured female bear.

She could barely hold herself up and relied on them to keep her standing.

"Tell us what you want, sweetheart," Carter said softly into her neck. They were all in on it, staying her orgasm, teasing her to death.

"I want to come," she cried. "Please, please, make me come."

Carter curled one arm around both her hands, imprisoning them behind her back and with his other hand he lifted her leg, parting her for his friends' view. "How? How do you want to come, sweetheart? You want Caleb's cock?" he asked. At that Caleb gripped his cock and stroked her pussy with it.

"Yes," she hissed. "Please." She tried to slip it inside her.

"What about Jack's cock, sweetheart? You want his too?"

"Please, please, please," she wailed when Jack guided his cock to her too. The sensation of having two thick, wet-with-pre-cum cocks stroking her up and down, between her lips and her clit threatened to blow her mind.

"What about mine?" Carter said, then slipped the head of his cock between her ass cheeks. He probed her hole and she crumbled. Her knees buckled, but they held her up.

"Please," she sobbed. Carter pushed in a little more, just at the entrance of her oh-so- thoroughly-cleaned hole. He was so much bigger than the butt plug Jack had put inside her. How could she be ready for this?

Jack parted her folds and dipped his cock in and out of her, but not deep enough. She needed them deeper inside her. All the way in. Caleb held his cock in his hand and rubbed against her clit, driving her mad.

They worked in unison. Jack would wet the tip of his cock with her wetness and spread it over her clit for Caleb who would stroke it with sometimes light, sometimes hard and fast strokes. Her body stiffened. Someone slapped and bit her nipple and then she was rattling out an orgasm that shook her soul. She sagged against Carter, weak and spent and trembling.

Jack lifted her up. She wrapped her legs around his waist as he carried her toward a low seated chair. But before he sat, he spun her around as if she weighed nothing so her back was against his chest and his cock nudged her ass. Her legs were spread wide across his thighs. Caleb and Carter stood before her, their gazes caressed her exposed pussy making it ache even more.

"Now, I want you to tilt forward until your hands are resting on the floor, kitten," Jack whispered in her ear.

"What?" she asked in a daze. Did he want her to do a wheelbarrow like thing—naked? Why was she still questioning them when they'd removed all her modesty already?

"Now, princess," Caleb instructed her. She lowered herself, Jack's arm around her waist kept her anchored until her palms rested on a cushion Carter had placed there for her. The position elongated her spine, dipped in at the base. Her legs were tucked on either side of Jack's lap, opening every intimate part of her for their viewing.

Carter and Caleb stood on either side of her. Helplessness ruled over her. The position they placed her in proved their dominance, their demands, their ability to do whatever they wanted with her.

Jack put his arm around her belly and brought her closer. The small strain in her shoulders became a necessary hardship for this experience. It couldn't be all pleasure. She needed some pain. She needed a fair amount of pain and discomfort. She had to prove her endurance. She would be rewarded then. She didn't know all these things before. She hadn't read about submission and domination. But what she did know, she knew from a space deep inside her. It came naturally. Maybe this was who she was.

They parted her wide, pulled her ass cheeks apart, ran their fingers into her pussy. First one finger than two, then three. They all had a finger each inside her as they pumped in and out of her. They used their hands to tap her clit and she cried at the contact. They rubbed and tweaked and thrust deep inside her and just as she was about to come, they slapped her clit making her lose her balance which earned her even harder smacks to her ass to straighten out her arms again.

They removed their hands and she heard them sucking her

juices from their fingers. Her wetness had spread all over their hands. Jack curled his arm around her belly again and brought her closer to him, and then his mouth opened on her.

"Please," she begged. Jack swept his tongue deep inside her then sucked on her pussy lips, pulling them taut which made her tummy do thrilling flips. Jack's tongue penetrated her again. Carter and Caleb tapped their cocks on her backside. Her body stiffened. She couldn't hold on. Liquid gushed out of her. Her orgasm felt like a thousand orgasms in one. Her legs shook. Her body shook.

She wasn't even finished with her climax, when Caleb took Jack's place. His tongue immediately swept over her. Her eyes bulged. He had just licked her hole. Her asshole. The sensation robbed her of thought, of time, of place. Caleb put a finger inside her then. He removed it and she couldn't be sure but either Carter or Jack poured lube into her hole and then all their fingers were inside her ass. Pumping her. So fast, and hard, Caleb had to keep an arm around her waist to keep her in place.

Could she come this way? She had to touch her pussy. She just had to. They were killing her by playing with her ass like that. She collapsed onto the side of her face, and with one hand reached between her legs, her clit crying for attention.

"Wrong move, kitten." Jack took her arm, then brought her hand to her lower back where he kept it. Her position now could not be more embarrassing. Total domination. She just prayed she didn't drool onto the pillow and take her humiliation all the way over the top.

She was being spanked now, the sound of strong, powerful hands on her soft butt echoed around the room. Their fingers fucked her so hard, so mercilessly. Her pussy leaked as it remained untouched, swollen like never before. Carter placed a hand on her pussy. The touch, so light, was more than enough to rock her off her axis and cause her to climax without shame. Without worry that she needed to the be pretty for them. With their fingers inside her backside, this orgasm was raw and vulgar and left her crazed and wild for their cocks.

*Good girl. You're fucking beautiful. Just gorgeous.*

She relished their praise but not for long. They removed their fingers. Her hand was released and she was told to balance on her palms again. More lube was poured into her. And then she felt the coolness of something round and small and foreign entering her behind.

# CHAPTER 11

"*K*now what we're doing to your pretty ass, princess?"

She couldn't see but she could feel. Another small ball entered her. She bit her lip. What were they doing to her?

"These are anal beads, sweetheart. We're going to stuff your ass, until you can't take anymore." Carter explained.

*Oh.*

Jack played with her pussy, the gushing sounds she made sent blood seeping to her cheeks. Another ball entered her. More lube was poured into her. She wasn't imagining it. The balls were getting bigger. The more balls Caleb entered, the more restless she became. She needed something, anything. She needed them.

"It's all right." Jack soothed her. "We're going to fuck you so good for taking this."

She whimpered. The ball Caleb was trying to push inside was too big. He stretched her. Carter held her cheeks apart, crooning at her.

"You can take this, sweetheart. Take this and I'll give you my cock. You want my cock, don't you, sweetheart?" She nodded. Past the ability to speak properly now.

"Relax, kitten." She listened to Jack. Let her muscles ease up. It required all her attention, all her concentration. Caleb popped the ball into her. She hissed and wanted to curse but held it in.

"You did amazing, princess." Caleb licked her hole again. Her back arched fully. She pressed her pussy into Jack's hand, trying to hump him. Trying to come.

"Not yet, sweetheart." Carter took Caleb's place. He slapped her ass-cheek, letting her flesh sizzle with heat. "We're going to make you even wilder, now."

With an arm around her waist, he brought her up into a sitting position on his lap. Jack and Caleb arranged her legs so that she was spread wide. Carter opened his long muscular legs even more, stretching her even farther. The balls in her ass made everything seem impossible and yet she realized just how hot and wet her pussy was when cool air drifted over it. But before long, Jack and Caleb were at her again. Caleb kneeled between her spread legs and Jack kneeled to one side of her. He tickled her clit then pulled really hard at it while Caleb engulfed the lips of her sex.

"Every time you resist coming, I'll take a ball out of you." Carter whispered in her ear.

What? What kind of weird pleasure trap was that? The balls inside her made her want to detonate from the inside out, and she would soon if Caleb and Jack kept touching her that way. Wouldn't less balls inside her mean less pleasure and that on top of not coming. Why? What was their game plan?

She shook her head, trying to tell them not to take the balls out of her and at once realizing she took as much torturous delight from her ass as she did her pussy.

"You don't want me to take out the balls? You like them inside you? You like having your asshole filled that way, sweetheart?"

She nodded. Shame refused to exist for her anymore.

"But what if I told you that after I take out the last ball because you resisted coming and then I will fill you with my cock. Wouldn't you want that? Wouldn't you want my cock which I can bury as deep as I want inside you? And fuck you. And come inside this lovely skinny-tight asshole of yours. Wouldn't you want that instead, sweetheart?"

She might have to black out. She couldn't deal with this over-load of sexual rawness that they were dishing out on her. But oh, how she wanted their cocks inside her. So badly, her life depended on it. She nodded furiously.

"Please, please, please!"

Jack slipped two fingers inside her and Caleb tongued her clit.

"You want my cock in your asshole, sweetheart?"

"Yes," she screeched as Jack entered three fingers into her, scis-soring them as Caleb played havoc with her clit. "Yes, please." Oh, god she was going to come. But she can't. Not if she wanted the reward of Carter's cock inside her ass.

She tried to push Jack and Caleb away. Carter caught her arms and held her tight. She tried to close her legs. They wouldn't let her. She wasn't going to make it. But at just that instant they released her and she breathed her orgasm away.

"Perfect," Carter said and pulled the biggest ball out of her. That in itself started her back on the path towards another orgasm. She thrashed and bit her lip and made incoherent sounds. But they didn't give her enough time to gather her wits before they were playing with her again. Carter fiddled with the string at the end of balls. Both Jack and Caleb had fingers inside her. Jack took her clit in his mouth and Caleb sucked on her inner thigh. This was it. She would ruin everything and come.

"What if I told you while I'm fucking your ass, either Jack or Caleb would fill this gorgeous pussy of yours with cock. Would you like that sweetheart? Two cocks inside you. In your tight and lovely ass and pussy?"

Fuck!

She screeched. Tears slid down her face. She begged them to stop. Begged for mercy. A tiny spasm started its way inside her. She growled and hissed and willed it away until they took pity on her and once again stopped touching her completely.

Carter removed another ball. She was getting emptier and emptier.

"Now, tell us. What's all that nonsense about you thinking you're undesirable? Tell us why you think that, sweetheart?"

No, please. If she told them, she might jinx it and they'd realize Paul was right and she wasn't worth it. "No, please. I don't want to," she whispered. Jack took a small whip to her breasts. The tassels stung her engorged nipples and the delicious pain ended with her pussy clenching.

"Talk," Caleb demanded. "Did someone tell you that you were undesirable?"

She shook her head. Jack brought his flogger down on her again.

"I... my ex-boyfriend—"

"Your ex-boyfriend? What's his name, kitten?"

She hesitated only because her mind had gone completely blank. To help her remember, Caleb bit her other nipple. That was enough to have her searching her brain so she could give them what they wanted so they would fuck her.

"Paul."

"Paul who? What's his surname, sweetheart?" Carter slapped her pussy. She quivered violently. They were only making it harder for her not to come, didn't they know that?

"Paul... Paul... Mc... Paul McAndrews," she blurted out his name.

"What did he say to you, princess?"

"He didn't say anything. Ooh." Carter removed one more ball from her ass. "He, he ran away after he, he penetrated me." For a second everyone stilled around her. She had broken the spell she had cast on them. Now they would know and act accordingly.

"What do you mean he ran away, kitten?" Jack asked softly leaving a trail of wet kisses along the side of her neck. Caleb now played with her nipples instead. Her breaths were harsh and loud and shameless. She stayed her orgasm but she still hovered precariously on the cliff.

"We were going to have sex for the first time, my first time. He put his thing inside me for a second and then took it out and fled without saying anything. I never saw him again. He left." She spoke every word in one long breath.

"And you think it's because you're undesirable? That's why he did that?" Carter asked.

"Yes," she said softly. *Please don't stop touching me.*

They started on her again. Fingers inside her. Mouths on her. Her pussy was slapped and pinched and sucked gently afterward and she loved it and it drove her insane and she forgot all about Paul.

"Do you have any idea how desirable you are to us, sweetheart? So desirable that we want you to have all our cocks inside you— two cocks inside your pussy, sweetheart, and one in your ass. Taking all three of us inside you that way, hmm, see how much we want you, how mad with lust you're driving us that we want to fuck you all at the same time? Would you like to do that eventually?"

She cried hopelessly with the need to come, and for the rewards she'd miss out on if she did. Yet she felt empowered. Their words and actions told her how much they wanted her. They'd bought her to impregnate her, not to have as their play thing, and yet they promised to play with her long and hard. She cried again because never had she been this needed. Jack stroked his cock, which was nearly bursting in his hand. And Caleb stroked his own. The blinding need for her she saw on their faces scared and delighted her. And Carter's cock continued to swell beneath her backside, wet with his pre-cum.

She wanted that so much. More liquid seeped out of her pussy. She couldn't think at all but for the thought of taking them all three inside her. Of her pleasing them that way. Of having the ability to please them.

Caleb brought something to her clit. Her eyes widened as she took in the toy. A wand. He turned it on and she kicked out her legs, wriggling on Carter's lap as Caleb entered two fingers into her. Her body slick with perspiration. She was going to come. Oh no.

But the rest happened so fast. Before her next breath, Carter pulled the last ball from her. She was lifted by Jack and Caleb as Carter drenched his cock in lube and then she was slowly lowered onto his cock. Holding his erection in hand, Carter guided it inside her. She sputtered out nonsensical words. The stretch burned. Nothing felt better.

"You're going to take my whole fucking cock, sweetheart. Every inch deep inside you."

"Yes, yes, oh please, yes!"

Carter grunted and brought her down fully on his cock. She froze. She hadn't expected this kind of fullness. She wasn't ready.

"You feel incredible. You're taking me sweetheart. All of me." She heard the agony in his voice, the restraint he used in allowing her to adjust. She glowed and moved. He growled in her ear and wrapped an arm around her, imprisoning both her arms. Jack took that damned toy to her clit again. He put it on some crazy speed setting and this time not one of them told her she couldn't come.

She earned this. She needed this. Her climax erupted with violent force. Wave after wave of contractions hit her. She made a mess. She must even look a bigger mess. Perspiration covering her body, her hair wild and untamed, her pussy dripping onto Caleb's thigh as he pushed his finger deeper inside. Her head dropped forward. She needed to compose herself. She couldn't look this savage in front of them.

"Fucking gorgeous," they murmured around her.

But all thoughts of making herself appear presentable disappeared when Caleb stood and guided his cock into her pussy. Slowly. Filling her up. She was going to burst. She couldn't take two cocks. But then Caleb started to move, in and out of her the same way Carter was in her ass. The combination, the rhythm, everything felt perfectly right and thoroughly dirty. She called for Jack and immediately he fed her his cock.

She sucked on him as Caleb and Carter fucked her. Another climax beckoned. They knew and started to pound into her even harder.

Her vision blurred. She removed Jack's cock from her mouth and held onto it tightly as she came again. Caleb curled his hand around her neck, this thrust deeper now, ever harder and faster. He growled.

"Saffron," he said hoarsely and came inside her. She loved it and clenched around him, milking him of everything he had in him. He slowed his pace after a while, lazily slipping in and out of her.

Jack removed her hand from his cock and swung his leg over her so that he straddled her, his cock in his hand, the fingers of the other gently caressing her clit. Carter ran his tongue down her neck.

"See how ready Jack is for you, sweetheart?"

She bit her lip and nodded. She wanted him inside her. She didn't want Caleb to leave her.

"Now, I need you to breathe, okay? Jack is going to take Caleb's place inside that incredibly wet pussy. Caleb's cum will work as lube and you'll be able to let him pass inside you, just for a second, all right? Just a taste of what it will be like when we stretch you enough to take two cocks in your pussy. Do you understand? Use your safeword if you can't manage it and don't worry. We'll be practicing on you a lot more so it's okay if this time it's too much for you. Saffron, sweetheart, do you understand?"

"Yes, Sir." Her body quivered with new need. She wanted so desperately to know what it would feel like to able to take all three of them inside her. She wanted to give them that so much.

Jack pushed in a little. Her breath caught. He rubbed her clit a little harder and kissed her lips softly.

"Just breathe, princess." Caleb slipped a little out and Jack pushed in. For one mind blowing moment they were both inside her, making her pant and feel wilder than ever. Jack kept up the play on her clit. The burning stretch in her pussy was complemented only by Carter slowing his pace and leisurely thrusting in and out of her. A thousand sensations raked over her. She grew very feverish and restless and started to move in that one second of having them both inside her as they passed each other. Caleb out of her and Jack in. After a moment, Jack fully took over where Caleb had once been.

"It's all right, sweetheart, we're going to go slow. That was just a little taste of how we're going to train you. How you're going to take two cocks inside you. You want that?"

"Yes, please. Please. I want it now."

"Soon, princess," Caleb said and gave her his cock to suck clean.

"Fuck, kitten, after that I don't think I can hold off for very long." Jack immediately started pounding into her. He stretched her thighs even further apart. Carter picked up his pace too. She was going to come again. God, she needed to climax. She needed it so badly.

"Come for us, kitten." Jack roared and stiffened and pumped into her.

"Fuck, I'm going to blow, sweetheart, right here in your ass."

That was all she needed. She held onto Caleb's cock for anchorage then gushed and grunted and thrashed as her orgasm hit. They held her fast and let her ride it out until she was completely and utterly spent. And couldn't move a single muscle.

She didn't have to do anything after that. They carried her into the tub filled with scented oils. She was lathered up by one of them. Dried and massaged by another and held until she slept half of the day away. She had entered a kind of paradise with them and loved every moment of it.

∼

It had been about a week since the night they first took her. And they'd taken her every night and morning and whenever else they could.

The night before after a tremendous night of fucking her, she broke her sleep and found Carter sitting in a chair staring at the moonlight. She went to him and curled in his lap. He wrapped his arms around her and she felt safe and protected from everything and anything.

Jack had opened up to her. He had told her about how his dad had nearly killed him the night of his fourteenth birthday. Both his parents beat him up, but that night his mother had been too drunk and his father not drunk enough.

As she sat in Carter's lap, being held so tightly by him, he thanked her.

"For what?" she asked.

"For being who you are. For accepting us. There was a woman once. We were with her for a one-night stand and she told Jack he looked sexier with his clothes on. That kind of messed with his confidence. Whenever we took a woman after that, Jack would not take his clothes off completely."

She had glanced at Jack at that very moment, sleeping, naked and glorious on the bed. Moments before that, he had taken her hard but slowly. She had kissed all his scars, had worshiped his body and then begged him to fuck her.

"And for Caleb?" Carter continued. "His father was a good man. He worked long and hard, but was away from home a lot. He tried to give his family everything. Caleb's real mother died at child birth and his stepmother hated Caleb. She would starve him and lock him in the basement. She hated him because her new husband loved him more than her. She told him he was gifted all right, but he was the gift you hated and threw away. He would carve out patterns in the wood in the dark to pass time."

Caleb did the paneling along the stairway. She had been certain it was Jack. Who knew.

"When his father died, he got put into foster care. All Caleb wants is for us to bring a child into this world and raise him with love and protection, like the love his father showed him. You're giving him that," Carter put his hand on her belly. "You're giving that to us, sweetheart. You're making it perfect for us because you are perfect."

Tears rolled down her face. She wanted nothing more than to give them the gift of a baby, something she had the power to do. "What about you?" she sniffed.

"Me? I was born an orphan. Been in the system practically all my childhood. When Caleb and Jack entered the system, I knew I had found my brothers. I protected them. I will always protect them."

She hugged him tightly. And fell asleep in his lap.

Now one week later, Carter was booming her name from downstairs.

"Saffron," he bellowed. "Come down here, sweetheart."

Oh, boy, what had she done now? Had she spoiled her trend of good girl spankings? No!

She rushed downstairs in jeans and a sweater and entered their study. At first, she didn't recognize the man who stood up when she entered. He looked familiar with his six-foot football player frame and short spiky blond hair. Only vaguely, though.

And then it hit her. Paul McAndrews. Her ex-boyfriend. What on earth was he doing here with them?

"You remember Paul?" Carter asked.

She swung her gaze from Carter to Caleb to Jack, all standing around or leaning nonchalantly into the furniture. The only person completely ill at ease was Paul. What the hell was going on?

"Do you, sweetheart?"

"I do." She frowned heavily at Carter.

"Well, Paul here has something to tell you, princess."

"I think you'd better hear him out, kitten," Jack smiled at her.

"Go ahead," Carter prompted.

"Saffron," Paul took a breath, "Saffron I wanted to apologize for, um, running out on you that night."

Oh no. Why was this being brought up now? She colored painfully.

"I'm sorry. It's just that you were the hottest girl at school and every guy I knew wanted to get with you and I, I kind of—"

She was so not the hottest girl. The most unpopular, definitely. The other girls didn't care much for the way she dressed or looked.

"Tell her what happened," Carter demanded of him.

"I had performance anxiety, okay?" Paul looked down, as flushed as she was.

And then it hit her.

"Oh my god." She glared at Carter. "You made him say that, didn't you?"

"Me? What kind of person do you think I am?" Carter asked gruffly, folding his arms, reminding her of the first time she saw him.

"A beast," she uttered, still incredulous. "Oh my god, you went and found him and made him say these things because you have to make everything right. It's what you do."

"No. I mean, they did find me, but it's true. I felt guilty for what I had done to you, Saffron, and I'm glad for this chance to apologize to you in person. But I didn't think I could tell you before because I'd ruin my reputation if it got out."

What was he saying? He was Paul McAndrews, his nickname was Melt, because he melted girls wherever he went.

"I didn't think… You were out of my league. And I'm very sorry for taking the coward's way out."

Saffron had to strain her legs to keep herself upright. All those years she had thought something was wrong with her. And yet it was this.

"I'm really sorry. Please accept my apology."

"I do and it's over, really. I was over it until you guys decided to bring it all back again."

"You deserved the apology, princess."

"You needed it, kitten."

Silence littered the room for a few seconds and then Paul came toward her.

"Look, Saffron, I want to make it up to you. If you're available and not dating anyone, I'd—"

"Okay, that's enough, buddy," Carter said. Paul looked completely confused when both Caleb and Jack took him by the back of his collar and started to escort him out.

"She's not available, pal," Caleb said.

"She's completely off limits," Jack said, emphasis on the word off.

"She's dating all right. All three of us," Carter finished as they shoved him out. "Show yourself out, will you," Carter called.

Saffron didn't know whether to laugh or be mad at them. She opted for something in between.

"Maybe I should go after him," she said saucily. "Maybe I want to date him. Maybe I was meant to have Paul 'Melt' McAndrews' baby after all."

Her words triggered a tsunami of testosterone in them which resulted in her being soundly spanked and thoroughly taken. There was nothing better than being taken by three jealous men who wanted to re-exert their authority over her.

# CHAPTER 12

*S*affron put her book down and stared out into the gray sky. She had been texting Marigold for hours, giving her just snippets of her life with the three men. She had had lunch lots of times with Marigold, here and at their house and their father had been to dinner here at least once a week. Her men had been more than gracious hosts. Marigold had told her their father was happier than he'd ever been and had stopped gambling altogether. He didn't relapse, not even once. Saffron could see his happiness on his face. He had taken up fishing now.

A smile played on her lips. Happiness and contentment filled her heart. Everything was going right. Her men were at work and her pussy clenched thinking of them coming home to her. She couldn't deny being a little disappointed when her period had arrived. She thought they might be disappointed in her, but they didn't even blink an eye. They fed her chocolate, rubbed her back, kept her feet warm and just pampered her. She had to laugh at how concerned they were for her when she was cramping. But the way they tended to her was the sweetest thing ever. She had passed her ovulation phase already and she wondered if this time she really did have their baby in her belly.

She prepared a meal for them for tonight. She wasn't a chef in any way but she had perfected the making of lasagna to an art form. She really couldn't wait for them to come home. Every night with them was unique and precious whether they made love to her, fucked her, spanked her, fed her, read to her or just held her.

She frowned at the sound of a car in the driveway. She got off the sofa and looked out the window and saw Tom, the man who worked for BHJ and was an acquaintance of her father and Montgomery. The same Tom who had driven her home after she stormed to their site to tell Jack what she thought of him avoiding her like that. That day had set everything into motion and had been the start of everything she now held dear. In that instant, her heart jerked and swelled.

She loved them. She had fallen in love with them. They were her whole life now. She never wanted to leave. She never wanted to live separately from them. She wanted to be with them until the day she died.

She opened the door for Tom, immediately pushing aside the worry that he'd come to tell her something had happened to one of them. She would have felt it, she was sure. Nothing would happen to them.

"Tom?" she asked frowning.

"Miss," Tom said. "Miss, I have some bad news." Tom's nervousness stretched across his face. His jaw twitched and he crushed his cap in his hands.

"What's wrong?"

"It's your father."

Saffron's knees almost gave way. She had just spoken to Marigold about him not so long ago. She had spoken to him last night herself and he seemed fine.

"You better read this, Miss." Tom handed her a piece of paper. She unfolded it and froze on the spot.

*Do as you're told and I won't cut off your father's head.*
*Montgomery*

"What? What is this?" she cried looking at Tom.

"He has your father. I'm to take you to him."

And something told her he wouldn't be allowing her to call his bosses.

"Please, Miss. He has my daughter. If you don't come with me right now he'll hurt her. I'm sorry," he said full of remorse. "I'm sorry," he repeated more to himself. "I knew I was playing with fire when I got involved with Montgomery. I can't let you contact anyone. Please, Miss, don't make me force you to come with me. I can't let him hurt my baby-girl."

Her blood boiling, Saffron wanted to rip Montgomery's head off. She knew she should leave a note for Carter. But she couldn't jeopardize Tom's daughter's life either. She would deal with that coward bastard Montgomery herself. His tactic of using people indebted to him to do his dirty work was over.

She sighed deeply. "Let me get a coat."

"No, Miss. I can't risk that. Please come with me now, I have twenty minutes to bring you back." The anguish on Tom's face broke her heart.

She went with him, her mind swirling with thoughts but nothing concrete came to pass as he drove them to a secluded cabin.

Montgomery stepped out of the door. She got out of the car.

"Where's my father?"

"Hey, pretty girl, that's not how you greet your new lover. Give me a kiss," Montgomery licked his lips.

"Screw you." She pushed past him and stepped into the cabin to see her father bound to a chair, his face bloody. She fumed with rage.

"What do you want?" she shouted.

"You. But first," he looked at one of three of his goons, "tie Tom up with his daughter. I can't release him and have him tell them where I'm keeping their girl. See how clever I am?" He smirked. Tom fought but was soon knocked out and taken to another room where Saffron got a glimpse of his daughter also tied to a chair.

"Now you and me, pretty woman, we're going to write those three sons of bitches a nice long letter. It's going to be fucking perfect. And if you don't write exactly what I say, I'm going to cut off your father's fingers one at a time until you do."

~

"Fuck," Jack roared.

"He lays a finger on her I swear I will take my time killing him," Caleb paced the floor.

"She's pregnant," Carter said quietly. He held the letter in his hand. Her handwriting. The pregnancy stick which came with the letter a moment ago lying on his desk.

*Dear guys,*

*I'm so sorry to do this to you but what can I say, you guys are the world's worst fools. You see you played right into my hand and my magic pussy. My boyfriend, Montgomery, came up with this plan from the start. Yes, you read that right, Thunder Montgomery and I have been lovers forever. I love him. He's the light of my life. Him and his ten-inch cock which I love and I suck all the time.*

*Anyway, back to the grand scheme. Now you see that three million you gave me, well that was to get me pregnant. And as you can see, surprise, it's a fucking baby, you fucktards.*

*Now, here's how brilliant my boyfriend, Thunder Montgomery, really is. Now that you know I'm pregnant, here's what's going to happen. You need to pay my boyfriend another three million if you want me to keep the baby. After all he's letting me keep some other fucker's baby. It's the least you can do.*

*You know, because my boyfriend, Thunder Montgomery, came up with this brilliant plan I think you should give him another mil—so that will be four million dollars.*

*See you soon, suckers.*

Carter skimmed the bank details below, also written in Saffron's handwriting and the number they had to call once the transfer was done for directions on where to come and pick Saffron up. If Montgomery thought for one second that any of them believed Saffron had been in on his plan the whole time, he was the goddamned fucktard. He didn't need to rage. In fact, he knew both Caleb and Jack kept their rage level the same as him. They were keeping it all for when they got their hands on Montgomery who had no idea who he had decided to play with. They didn't grow up in the system to be soft and easy. Not one of them was soft or easy. That kind of hardness would stay with them forever. They just knew how to channel their darkness.

But fuck, was she really pregnant?

"We find her and bring her back home. And we end Montgomery for daring to even breathe the same air as her."

SAFFRON FELT ILL. Everything had happened so fast. How did her day go from being blissfully happy to this new nightmare in a few hours? She tried to tend to her father, who kept mumbling around his gag.

She couldn't be mad at him because he had left his gambling habits behind and had turned over a new leaf in his life. She was sorry, too because now he had to get dragged back into Montgomery's warped world.

She had hated writing that stupid letter. One of his idiot men held a set of pliers to her father's fingernails. A starting point, he had called it.

She hated how they would feel when they read it. Would they believe she'd been in on it from the start? Would they think she had deceived them once again? Tears welled up inside her, but she refused to cry in front of Montgomery.

She had no clue what was going to happen to her. Would

Carter, Caleb, and Jack decide she just wasn't worth the trouble and ignore the note. The thought of never seeing them again, of being discarded by them after she had fallen in love with all three of them killed a massive chunk of her heart. Hours had gone by since the letter was delivered. And oh god, the pregnancy test showing positive. They hadn't yet called, and there were only three hours to arrange the money and call. They had to call in the next fifteen minutes or something fatal was going to happen.

"You want to cry, beautiful?" Montgomery broke out into foul laughter that made her feel like retching. "Fucking hell. You want to cry over those fucking men?" He came to her as she kneeled by her father. He gripped her hair hard, pulled and then shoved her away.

"You don't know who you're messing with," she said, keeping the tremble from her voice.

"Oh, I don't know who I'm messing with," he mimicked her. "Those rich soft pretty boys? I'll have them dead before they can say, well, before they can say anything.

Saffron shook her head. "You don't know anything about them," she said quietly.

"Oh yeah? What about you? What do I know about you? You're nothing but a whore," he spat her at. She glared at him, murder in her eyes. "Oh, you don't think so? You think they love you, they want to marry you? Fuck that. They fucking paid to fuck you. Now, what do you think that makes you? Huh? That's a whore in everyone's book, sugar. They don't love you. You think those rich bastards give a fuck about you? Think again. They're going to pay my money because all they want is a baby. You, you're just a vessel. A good time whore. They don't love you. You mean nothing to them. I'll say it again, don't think they're saving you by paying up. They're saving their fucking baby. You will always be their very expensive whore."

Saffron looked down. Her father murmured something, but he was gagged and Montgomery refused to remove it. Was it true? Were they only interested in their child. How would she ever know.

Tears rolled down freely now and Montgomery laughed all the more.

"You know I'm right. Join me and we'll spend those fuckers' money and make our own babies."

Montgomery's voice died down. If she thought her day had been a speeding unstoppable train-wreck, what happened in those next moments was a blitz of lightning. She replayed bits of what she'd seen in her head. Carter, Caleb, and Jack kicking the door in. Jack and Caleb took care of the Montgomery's sidekicks and soon they were lying unconscious in a heap on the floor, their knives and guns taken from them.

Carter had Montgomery in a tight grip, Montgomery's own knife positioned dangerously at his throat.

"Don't ever fuck with what's ours," Carter said. The menace and fury in his voice only matched by the expressions on Jack's and Caleb's faces. But for one glorious moment, when their gazes met, hers with theirs, the relief that she wasn't hurt shone through and she felt loved and cherished and protected. She had never seen them that vulnerable even if it were only for a few seconds.

Jack and Caleb came to her and picked her up, inspecting her as if she were precious cargo. She assured them she was fine, but they were only satisfied after an inspection and then they nodded to Carter.

She couldn't walk. She felt weak. They'd overwhelmed her, stunned her. They were here. They came. They didn't discard her. Jack scooped her up as Caleb untied her father and released Tom, and his daughter who had been hit in the face by Montgomery or one of his men from the other room.

Sirens wailed in the background and soon a male and female officer came onto the scene. She was passed onto the female officer, but she didn't want to leave.

"It's all right, princess." Caleb held her by the arms. "Officer Smith will take you and your dad to the hospital. She's not going to leave you until we're there. You're safe now."

She was torn between getting her father seen to and not wanting to be away from the three of them. "But what about you and Carter and Jack?"

"We'll see you in a bit, kitten. It's going to be okay."

"We're just going to stay behind and have a little chat with Montgomery, maybe teach him some manners. Like never to fuck with what belongs to us." Carter's knife pressed into his throat. "Get your dad seen to, sweetheart. We'll all be home soon."

The male officer ushered Tom and his daughter away. Officer Smith guided her father out and after nodding, she followed. Montgomery clearly whimpered when both officers left him alone with Carter, Caleb, and Jack.

EXCEPT for a swollen lip and bruised cheeks, her father was perfectly fine everywhere else. He was released after he was treated. Marigold rushed to the hospital and after Saffron explained what had happened, she knew she had to get that horrible weight off her heart immediately. Officer Smith then drove her to the house where she had found and maybe lost the loves of her lives.

"Are you okay, Saffron?" The officer asked as they entered the house. She had told Saffron she was going to text Carter to tell him she was taking Saffron to their house.

"I'm fine," Saffron smiled. She wasn't really. Montgomery's words kept playing in her head. Would they ever love her? Love someone they paid for? "I think I'll take a shower. Please help your-self to anything in the kitchen."

Saffron took a long hot shower and slipped into a pair of jeans and a tank top. She slung a long heavy sweater over her shoulders. She then proceeded to pack her things. She cleared the room of all her belongings then carried her bags down the stairs.

They still weren't home yet. She wanted to know what they did to Montgomery. And how much power did they have if even the cops left them alone to take care of him themselves. And how did they find her?

Officer Smith said nothing of the bags she brought with her into the lounge and Saffron was grateful. If she uttered one word she would never stop crying.

Evening came quickly as she sat by the window waiting for them. Officer Smith sat companionably quiet and sipped tea which she also made for Saffron. But the reason they came back for her, the real reason weighed her down. Her or the baby?

Her heart missed a beat when she heard them. Officer Smith came to her and hugged her and said she'd be all right, that whatever was troubling her could be fixed or it would pass too. It was only her whole life, Saffron mused. Officer Smith then left her in the lounge while she went to meet the men in the foyer.

She heard them say goodbye hurriedly to the officer and then heard the door shut.

She was going to faint. She couldn't face them. How on earth was she going to pay their three million back? She couldn't take it back from Marigold and her father. It was all her fault for falling in love with them. But she would promise them she would work until the day she died to pay them back.

Her anxiety increased with every passing second. She couldn't tell them the truth. She didn't want to learn the real reason they rescued her. They charged into the lounge, ready to take her into their arms. But she couldn't let them.

"Choke," she whispered her safeword. And they stopped dead in their tracks, their gazes wide and confused.

"Saffron? What's going on?" Carter asked.

They immediately spotted her bags. Heavy frowns crossed their brows. How she loved these men. All three of them. She needed all three of them to make her feel whole.

"Is this because of that letter, princess?"

"Because we know it's not true. We know you weren't trying to scam us. We know that, kitten."

"How did you find me?" Montgomery tried to keep her location a secret and since they hadn't called him for directions, how could they know where she'd been?

"By whatever means we could. In case you hadn't realized this already, we're very powerful men, sweetheart. Those of Montgomery's men who refused to talk after we bribed them soon realized they should have taken the money in the first place. There was no way we wouldn't have found you." They moved toward her again.

"Please, no. Choke," she said going backward. She never doubted they would think she was involved with Montgomery. That wasn't what was drowning her in misery.

"What the fuck is going on, Saffron?" Carter asked.

"I'm sorry." Oh no. Her tears broke free and she wept. "I'm sorry. I'm not… I'm not pregnant."

"What?" Caleb asked.

"Montgomery made me take a pregnancy test and it was negative and then he got one of his sidekicks to get him a pregnancy test that showed positive to let you think I was pregnant. So that you would save me because you only wanted a baby from me, you paid me to have your baby."

"Damn right we paid you," Jack exploded. "We would pay you every last fucking cent we have. We would pay you with the world to have our baby, Saffron, we would do anything for you, for you to have our baby."

"But I'm not pregnant and if you knew I wasn't, you wouldn't have—"

"Don't you dare finish that sentence, princess. We're determined to spend the rest of our useless fucking lives saving you, you're all that matters, Saffron. Only you," Caleb said.

"Do you know what we were doing three days ago?" Carter said. "We went to see a jeweler. We have a receipt to prove it. Do you know why we're so late coming back home after shipping Montgomery off to do some hard labor on a friend's plantation right on the other side of the world, with no money and passport? It was either that or kill him. We chose the least messy solution, but do you know why we're late? We went to see your father, to ask him permission. Saffron, sweetheart, we want to marry you. We want to make you our wife, ours in everything and we didn't care whether you were pregnant or not, sweetheart. Fuck, we love you. We're in love with you."

"Do you hear that? We're in love with you. We want you to be our wife, princess, pregnant or not."

"You made us break all our rules, kitten, never fall for a woman. Not with the kind of lives we've lived. But you broke into our hearts and fuck you've become the only reason we need now to do anything. To live and breathe. We're in love with you, kitten, in love with every inch of you and you alone, pregnant or not."

"Will you marry us, Saffron. Will you take us as your husbands, your protectors, your champions for the rest of your life because that's all we want, we want you forever."

She was such a mess, sobbing uncontrollably. Was she dreaming?

## CHAPTER 13

$S$he wasn't dreaming. This was real. This was happening.

"Say yes," Jack whispered.

"Please, say yes," Caleb added.

She nodded and ran to them and was kissed and held and told how much she was loved. She was stripped naked lovingly. Caleb went behind her and tugged her jeans and panties off in one go. And when he rose, he cupped her pussy as Jack divested her of sweater and tank top. Her whole body was kissed, from her toes to the top of her head. She felt so cherished, so treasured. They held her with delicate touches and their kisses were beautiful and long and sweet.

"Be our wife."

They each took a box out of their pockets. She was sobbing again.

They slipped three beautiful rings onto her finger and they all clasped together to make one. She was so happy she thought she might burst.

"Thank you," she whispered.

"We haven't earned that thanks yet, sweetheart," Carter said darkly. Her pussy had been pleasantly wet, hungering to take them inside her, but now her wetness flowed. Her nipples hardened even more.

"We need to teach you again to know who you belong to. And the only way to do that is to fuck you until you can't walk and spank you until you can't sit," Caleb said.

"While we refresh your memory as to who you belong to, the only thing you're going to be wearing for the next week at least are our rings," Jack added.

"What do you say, sweetheart?"

"Yes, Sir. Please teach me who I belong to. Please," she ended her almost pathetic plea.

Carter then picked her up and carried her to their bedroom. He threw her onto the bed and she bounced, then sat and kneeled as she watched them undress. Their cocks were enormous and ready to punish her for thinking she could walk away from them just like that. Her breath caught. Her pussy vibrated with need.

"You need reminding about who fucking owns you?" Carter growled as he pushed her back onto the bed, clutched the backs of her knees and brought her to the edge of the bed. He spread her wide then slapped her thigh really hard.

She quaked. "Yes, Sir, I do," Saffron squeaked.

"Who owns you?" he growled again and shoved his cock into her so deep and hard and full she forgot to breathe for a few seconds. "Who owns you?" he asked again.

"My men, Sir. My men own me." She was dripping and needed to touch her clit. She sneaked her hand down. Carter's heavy thrusts sent her up and down the down. Jack caught her arm, then Caleb caught her other arm and stretched it over her head. They kneeled on either side of her face and fed her both their cocks at the same time.

"We own you, don't we, princess?"

"You belong to us. Every part of you belongs to us. Your mouth, your ass, your pussy, your whole body is ours, kitten. Don't ever forget that."

The instant she tasted their pre-cum her orgasm ripped through her. Carter slapped her clit and she cried out and tried to squeeze her thighs shut. But Caleb held both sides of her head now.

"Open your mouth, princess," he ordered. She parted her lips and kept her gaze on him. He played with her. She was already beginning to salivate. Jack whipped her nipple with his cock then leaned down and drew her nipple between his teeth. Carter increased his pace inside her. Caleb still toyed with her, letting her keep her mouth open for his cock. Jack bit down a little harder on her nipple and she felt another orgasm starting its downward spiral.

"You're ours, princess. Ours," Caleb said and slid his cock into her mouth. She gagged but she refused to give him up. Jack left her nipple and she moaned the loss. For a second, she was empty when Carter pulled out of her, but then Jack filled the space and everything was right again. She held onto Carter's cock until Caleb forced her to release him. He then played with her nipples as she sucked all her juices off Carter's cock.

As Jack pounded into her he played with her clit, teasing another climax from her. She was going crazy. She loved them so much. She grew restless. She didn't know how to prove her love for them. That fever that they ignited raged inside her and at once she knew what she wanted.

"Please, please…" she begged. She found it hard to articulate what she wanted. She was an emotional and sexually turned on mess with a mission to prove her love for three men who became her world. Her universe. Her end.

"What do you want, kitten?"

"I want… please… Please I need… I need you inside me. I need all three of you inside me, please."

They had played and stretched her pussy so she could take two of their cocks inside her. She always felt stretched beyond her limit. But they always made her so wet she couldn't string words together.

Jack slipped out of her. Carter stilled. So did Caleb.

"You're not ready," Carter said.

"It doesn't matter, please." She sat up on her knees. They all stood together now around the bed. "Please. I love you all. And I want to do this. Please don't say no. I can take it. I know I can."

"She's so fucking tight with two of us already," Caleb said.

"We could hurt her," Jack said.

"You won't. You know how to do this. You know what's best for me. Please." She begged. They didn't look as if they would approve her request. "I want to have your baby, and please this is how I want to have your baby. Just this once, please. I can do this if you'll let me. I don't have anything to give you."

"Sweetheart."

"No. It's true. I don't have anything of value to give you." She glanced at her beautiful ring. She wasn't stupid, she knew it cost the price of an island. "I'm not talented in anything. I don't have a career. For so long I didn't know what I wanted to do with my life. But now I know. I want to do you three. I am destined to love you —and I won't ever retire from that job, not until I die and even after. This is my life, you three are. And having you all three inside me, so I can give a you baby, that's the only thing I can give you. Please, take it. It's not much, but it's me begging for a chance to prove how much I love you. This is all I have. My body."

"Fuck," Caleb said softly.

Jack's Adam's apple bobbed and Carter rubbed his hand over his head.

"Please take me." She was crying now. Their silence killed her.

"We go in slow, but firm, and we come out fast," Carter said. "Come here, sweetheart. Let's get you as wet as possible."

She lay on her back and spread her thighs for them. Caleb's hands gripped her as he licked her. Jack joined him and filled her with his fingers. Carter lay by her side, kissing her.

"We're going to take you close to orgasm and then stop a few times. And then we're going fuck you, all right, sweetheart?"

She nodded. She understood. They were just going to come inside her as quickly as possible. "Shouldn't I suck you?" She stopped then arched her back as Jack manipulated her clit with his teeth and Caleb's fingers curled into her G-spot. And then everything was stopped again "Shouldn't I suck your cocks first?" she tried again, suddenly shy and turned on and just so insanely in love with them.

"No, sweetheart," Carter said at the same time Jack and Caleb went back into her pussy. "We'll be fine. Just the thought of having all three of us inside you will make us blow very quickly. You still sure you want this?"

"Oh god, yes," she screamed. Another climax threatened to make landfall, and then was stopped. She was so wet the sheet under her had to soak some of her wetness up. "No more. Please, now, now. I need it now. Please, Carter. Please."

She could have shouted her relief when they started to lube up their cocks and pour even more into her. They acted fast. She couldn't be more grateful. Carter made her straddle him. His cock slid in and she dropped her head onto his shoulder as some of her angst was released. Caleb slipped in from behind her and his cock inched in. She gasped like she always did. Now she only needed Jack. Sweet, sweet Jack.

He climbed over her and his weight on her immediately offered her solace.

"You all right?" Carter asked.

She nodded. And smiled.

She imagined how Jack was gripping his cock as he guided it into her. He probed and she squirmed. But he didn't relent. He pushed in further. Carter and Caleb lay still inside her as they encouraged her, told her how beautiful she was. How amazing this gift was that she was giving them.

Jack pushed more. The stretch started to get real. She whimpered, breathing through her nose. Carter licked her nipples. Caleb caressed her thighs. Jack pushed in more. She bit back a raw scream and wriggled around. Oh god.

"Do you want us to stop, sweetheart?"

"No," she shook head, grunting hard, panting wildly. "No, don't stop. Just do it now, please. I want to feel you all inside me, please."

Carter held her tight as Jack pushed in as much as he could. She shouted and moaned and shattered. Caleb started to move inside her. He snaked his hand between their bodies and found her clit. Carter nipped and sucked her nipples. Jack took a grip of her hair and pulled. She groaned at the sensation in her scalp. At the delicious pleasure and pain in her pussy.

Those were exactly the sensations to take her over the edge. Pain and pleasure and protection. They gave her all three. And now she was bursting with it.

"I love you," she cried, tears streaming down her face as she bit her lip. "I love you all so much." It should have been impossible, but her men grew larger inside her.

"Now. Come inside her now."

She was gripped even tighter, smothered by the warmth and strength of three beautiful bodies. She became everything they wanted. Their grunts and curses and her name falling from their lips like a prayer made her glow and find a kind of peace that was unearthly.

Their bodies stiffened. Their cocks inside her grew even harder. Wetness washed into her. So much. She cried with joy that she had done this. For them.

They pulled out of her slowly, more exhausted than they'd ever been. She knew they normally took her really hard, and very fast and sometimes if she was really good, very rough. But this time they showed restraint. They fucked her gently, but not for too long. They were constantly aware of her well-being and they trusted Carter to call it off at once if it became too much for her. She couldn't stop smiling. Yes, her vagina felt slightly sore, but really she never wanted that pain to go away. It would always remind her how much they cherished her and loved her.

She immediately lay on her back with feet in the air against the headboard. She heard Jack's chuckle. There were mixed reviews about this method for ensuring pregnancy, but she'd do anything. Jack came to her and kissed her upside down. His hand splayed out on her belly then gently cupped her sex.

"Thank you, kitten," he said. She curled her hand around his head and kissed him.

"I love you, Jack Hallson," she said.

He smiled and returned the words to her then dropped his head next to hers. His legs facing the opposite direction from hers.

Carter came to her next and kissed her. He touched her belly and cupped her pussy. "Thank you, sweetheart," he said.

She curled her hand around his head too and kissed him deeply. "I love you, Carter Blake," she said. He responded with the same, his head on the other side of her.

Caleb came to her at last. "Thank you, princess," he said, and his hand slid down her belly to her pussy where he cupped her. She brought him closer and kissed him again.

"I love you, Caleb Jeffries," she said. He said the same to her and dropped down on the bed so the top of his head touched the top of hers. Perfect.

She smiled and she could feel their smiles, too.

The best day of her life had started the moment she beat her sister at the toss of a coin. These men were her destiny. She closed her eyes and dreamed of a baby for the lumberjacks.

# EPILOGUE

NIGHT MONTHS LATER....

Saffron held the little baby girl in her arms. With her riot of dark baby hair and big brown eyes, her husbands declared she was the spitting image of her mother. Saffron became flushed thinking about her men. She had never seen them more stressed than when she went into labor, including Jack who was a doctor. Even though her contractions were killing her, she made sure to laugh at them in between each one. She was of course threatened with a severe spanking once she recovered.

She remembered the night this little darling was conceived. How amazingly gentle they'd been with her. How she had to beg to make them all three come inside her. They showered her with a never ending supply of gifts after that because of the gift she had given them. She wanted for nothing and if she only had the three of them she would still be the richest woman alive.

"Your daddies are coming soon to take us home, little one," she whispered to her daughter. Saffron's father and her sister Marigold had just left a couple of minutes ago. "They've probably padded up the whole house so you never hurt yourself. You have no idea, but we're the luckiest girls in the world."

Just then the door opened and in strode her husbands. Tall, with the brute strength and sheer size of a true lumberjack. The same dizzying sensations their presence brought her from the moment she first laid her gaze on them glided over her. She had fallen in love with them from the very first moment. How could she not.

She couldn't wait to recover so she could feel their power inside her again until she was bursting with their love for her.

The End

## CHLOE KENT

Chloe Kent has been hooked on romance since her teens and couldn't wait to grow up and write her own romance novels. Her books usually feature a spirited heroine, and at least two... sometimes more incredibly hot heroes.

Her favorites pastimes include her husband, her dog, and books. Her biggest fear is running out of coffee or her imagination.

Visit her blog here: http://chloekentblogs.blogspot.co.za/
Find her on Facebook: https://www.
facebook.com/chloekentbooks
Find her on Twitter: @ChloeKentBooks

*Don't miss these exciting titles by Chloe Kent and Blushing Books!*

Her Alaskan Men
A Baby for the Lumberjacks
Their Boss's Daughter

Printed in the USA
CPSIA information can be obtained
at www.ICGtesting.com
LVHW050426160823
755199LV00067B/496